FERAL
PRIDE

FERAL
PRIDE

CYNTHIA LEITICH SMITH

CANDLEWICK PRESS

The epigraph that appears on page vii originally appeared in *Jungles* and is provided courtesy of Frans Lanting.

First edition 2015

Library of Congress Catalog Card Number 2014944625
ISBN 978-0-7636-5911-0

14 15 16 17 18 19 BVG 10 9 8 7 6 5 4 3 2 1

Printed in Berryville, VA, U.S.A.

This book was typeset in Minion Pro.

Candlewick Press
99 Dover Street
Somerville, Massachusetts 02144

visit us at www.candlewick.com

For Aunt Linda,
whose encouragement and pride in my efforts
inspires me to roar

"... A LION IS NOT A LION IS NOT A LION.
AS INDIVIDUALS, AS MEMBERS OF A SOCIETY,
THEY'RE ALL VERY DIFFERENT."

— FRANS LANTING, WILDLIFE PHOTOGRAPHER

Austin News Channel
Transcript: April 21

Anchor: This just in! The following video was taken with a night-vision camera in Pine Ridge, Texas (population 7,394), located about an hour southeast of Austin.

That figure contorting on your screen is believed to be an actual werecat, caught in mid-shift at Town Park—a public park located in the shadow of the historic downtown, along the Colorado River. She has been identified as Kayla Morgan, a senior at Pine Ridge High, a National Merit semifinalist, a track and cross-country state champion, and the adopted daughter of Mayor Franklin Morgan.

The structure in the background is an antique Western-themed carousel, which was the site of the death of PRHS quarterback Benjamin Bloom—from a lightning strike—back in February. We have confirmed that Kayla and Benjamin were dating at the time.

If you look closely, you can see other, as yet unidentified, individuals in the background. It appears as though at least one of them is a werecat, too. While shifters have been caught on video before, it's extremely rare and unprecedented in small-town Texas.

The Bastrop County Sheriff's Office has just issued a statement saying—quote—"Kayla Morgan and her companions are suspected of no known crimes. Nor are they suspected of having any connection whatsoever to the kidnapping of Texas governor Linnie Lawson.

Kayla's species has not been verified."

CLYDE

I WON'T BE CAGED. Not again. I tense at the crackle of the police radio. I check the side mirror. Not yet. I rub my eyelids, look again. I'm not the only one who's freaking out. The stink of shock and fear is weighty. I can hear my girlfriend Aimee's heart thudding in her chest.

"None of this makes sense," Kayla says from the backseat of the squad car. "It's not illegal to be what we are. Why would federal agents be gunning for us?"

"Why wouldn't they?" answers Yoshi, who's beside her.

They're both right. It's not illegal to be what we are. But whenever anything goes wrong, anything bloody and brutal, shape-shifters are presumed guilty. So, what went wrong this time?

Behind the wheel, Jess says, "Sure, there's the footage. Werepeople in small-town America, cue the hysteria. But the feds were already after y'all before it went live."

Earlier tonight Kayla's shift to Cat form (and possibly Yoshi's, too) was caught on video. It was uploaded to the International News Network and beyond. She's become the latest poster child for shifters as beastly boogeymen. Meanwhile, shoot-first feds descended on Town Park. I'd already swept up Aimee. We'd taken refuge in a heavily wooded area nearby. But Kayla and Yoshi were momentarily arrested. A Coyote named Peter and a wereotter named Evan managed to escape. Darby, a Deer, was knocked unconscious and left behind with Tanya, a Bear. An elder werecat, Lula Stubblefield, ran into the line of fire to distract the armed SOBs. We've all been doing a bang-up job of avoiding the topic of her death.

The Cats had just transformed back to human form when the Federal Humanity Protection Unit (FHPU) started shooting. There was no time for them to waste getting dressed, and we've been on the run since. That's why they're both buck naked and handcuffed.

Fortunately, shifters have human allies like Aimee and Kayla's friend Jess, who came to our rescue in her father's squad car. Her dad, the local sheriff, helped finagle our escape.

That was about an hour ago. Now, it's nearly one in the

morning. Traffic on the interstate is light. Aimee flicks a downward glance. "You okay?"

I whisper, "It's nothing." Well, not *nothing*, but . . . She's perched on my lap in the bucket seat. It's not just that I'm a teenage guy. Or just that she's my girlfriend. I briefly bulked up my muscle mass and fur back in Pine Ridge. A bigger package is part of the deal. That's not discussed in mixed company. Again, Aimee's not only female. She's a *Homo sapiens.*

Normally, Yoshi would be listening in and mouthing off about my predicament. But Kayla's Chihuahua won't shut up. "Peso can't help it," she insists. "Be nice to him. He gets carsick sometimes."

"He's going to ralph all over my lap!" Yoshi exclaims. All Cats are fastidious. Yoshi's a metrosexual. "That's it!" he says. "Jess, pull over. Nobody's chasing us right this second. We've got to get these cuffs off. Clyde, you give Kayla your shirt."

"We should've thought of that," Aimee mutters, which is her nice way of saying that *I* should've thought of that. Kayla was adopted by the human mayor of Pine Ridge and his missus. She's less comfortable au naturel than any shifter I've met before.

Yoshi's after her, which is a relief. For a while, he'd set his sights on Aimee.

"Next exit," Jess promises, hitting the wiper fluid. "I'll

5

find a secluded spot."

Aimee begins squirming, which doesn't help my situation. I ask, "What're you doing?"

She checks her pockets. "Looking for the keys to the handcuffs."

"You *lost* the keys?" Kayla exclaims.

They slipped, unnoticed, through Aimee's fingers as she positioned herself on my lap. With my werelion-wereopossum reflexes, I snatched them in midair.

"Check the floorboard," Jess says to Aimee. "You probably dropped them."

Yoshi kicks the back of my seat. "What the hell, Clyde!"

The Cats' wrists are restrained behind them. We've had a long night. There's no way Yoshi's comfortable like that. He might be suffering from a little awkwardness of his own, with no jeans to hide it. But notice how he goes straight for blaming me.

Because why? Yoshi's a senior. I'm a sophomore. He's been all Cat his whole life. After being raised by Possums as a Possum, I've only recently discovered my inner Lion.

Yoshi is Mr. Smooth with the ladies. Me? Not so much. He's become Aimee's closest guy friend, like I need that in my life.

I'm not ashamed to be half wereopossum. It's the animal form I've exclusively identified myself with for most of my life. But Possums aren't considered the sexiest. Or even sexy-ish.

I'm a Wild Card, dual species. Based on grocery-store paperbacks, it seems like werecurious human girls fantasize about lean predators like Wolves and Cats. Bears, if they're into the husky type. Aimee and I clicked back when I thought of myself as strictly weremarsupial. We didn't go from friends to more until after I learned how to roar.

Yoshi kicks the back of my seat again. I squeeze the keys in my palm. Aimee rushes to apologize. As Jess accelerates past the next exit, my girlfriend insists she's at fault.

I'm pissed enough at Yoshi to let her.

YOSHI

HOURS BEFORE SUNRISE, fleeing Texas in an ungodly crowded police car, the only thing my friends can talk about is Wonder Woman. "Diana represents one-third of the DCU Trinity, and who's her archenemy?" Kayla asks. "Cheetah. Not only a werecat, but a spotted werecat."

At least she's speaking up. A spotted werecat herself, Kayla's a lot quieter when she's naked. Self-conscious, I guess. Religious. Not me. I'm a dashing, cougar-like Cat myself with jet-black fur in animal form. I love my body.

"This is significant . . . why?" Jess asks from behind the wheel. Like everybody else up front, she has her clothes on. "Shifters are people. There are terrific people, terrible people. Most fall in between. Why can't a wereperson be a villain? Because the hero is Wonder Woman?"

"Wereperson" is a sometimes preferred term for "shifter." (I don't mind either one, so long as nobody's calling me a "freak of nature" or a "monster" . . . or insulting my hair.) We're in no way supernatural, even if our bodies can perform a few tricks that are beyond our human cousins. We're no recent mutation either. We trace our evolutionary line back to at least the Ice Age.

That's not breaking news. Werecats and, for that matter, werewolves and weredeer and Raccoons and Vultures (among others) have been common knowledge among *Homo sapiens* since the mid-1800s. Some humans, like Jess and Aimee, are cool with us, but the rest . . . not so much. The not-so-much crowd, they're the majority. Or at least they're louder.

The great thing about being in a cop car is that other vehicles give us wide berth. I don't like it, though, Aimee sitting on Clyde's lap with the seat belt stretched across them. We're doing seventy-five miles per hour, and I've only got one best friend. She'd be safer back here. It's cramped but she's tiny, and it's not like she has to touch my naked bod — not that I'd blame Clyde for objecting. (I am irresistible.) She could sit on the other side of Kayla. That would press the Cat girl tight against me. Nudity before and after shifts isn't a big deal among werepeople. But this is *Kayla*. I should be getting more credit for not staring at her rack. Like a ticker-tape parade.

"Clyde, what did I tell you?" Jess moves to the far right lane to let a camper trailer pass.

"Don't touch the center console," he replies with a sigh. He's such a baby. He keeps playing with the radio, camera, and light-bar controls. Which, granted, are pretty cool.

We debated taking back roads (or at least avoiding tolls), but ultimately decided that I-35 North, the fastest route to Oklahoma, was worth the risks. Not for the first time, I strain against the cuffs and feel the metal give a bit. If I had the strength of a werebear, I'd be free by now.

Kayla and I discussed trying to shift ourselves free, but trapped in this position, my head bent from the low ceiling, our arms restrained behind our backs — no way. That's not superficial, stage-one stuff — like fur, eyes, claws, teeth. We could throw a joint out of socket or puncture a lung with a rib bone. We've got it made over humans when it comes to healing (when our forms shift, we largely reboot ourselves), but bone and organ injuries are tougher to repair than flesh.

"Werepeople are portrayed as archvillains a lot," Aimee points out. "Cheetah isn't supposed to be an *Acinonyx jubatus sapiens* like Kayla, but I doubt most Wonder Woman fans put much thought into the difference." Are we *still* talking about this?

The squad car has been pro cleaned, but somebody threw up in this backseat within the past couple of weeks. I'm getting a headache, and it's not helping that Kayla's Chihuahua won't shut up. Most small animals panic in the presence of werepredators. It's novel that, because he's Kayla's, Peso is so comfortable around us. Still, we should've left him in Pine Ridge. If he scrambles over my junk one more time, I swear . . .

"Better an archvillain than a sorry-ass villain," Clyde chimes in, scratching his freshly grown beard. He's a Wild Card shifter, half Lion, half Possum (he can choose between forms).

Staying clean-shaven is key to passing as human, at least until we're out of high school. Passing — hiding in plain sight in human form — is the way most of us survive. Especially urban shifters, but even country boys (like I used to be) do their best to act average. There are species-only communities like Wolf packs, but Cats are too independent for that sort of BS.

"Besides," Clyde goes on, "Cheetah started out as a pathetic *Homo sapiens* woman in a cat suit. It helped enormously to reinvent her like that. Think about it: How could some random society babe with a personality disorder pose a serious challenge to Diana?"

They do that all the time — or at least Aimee and Clyde do — they talk about superheroes and sci-fi characters like they're on a first-name basis. For hours . . . this has been going on *for hours*. I'm finally bored enough to join in. "You'd sign off on a random society dude with a personality disorder challenging her."

"Would not!" Clyde exclaims. "I bow to the awesomeness that is the Amazon princess."

"What if it was Bruce Wayne?" I counter as a trio of motorcycle riders cruises by. "Society dude. Major issues. If he's Superman's fail-safe, shouldn't he be able to take down Wonder Woman, too?" That shuts him up. I'm not a geek, but I hear them jabber about this stuff all the time. It seemed like the thing to say to score points with the girls.

Besides, this whole conversation is whistling in the dark — talking about anything except what's really wrong. We're retreating to safety. Wolves would stand their ground and fight, but Wolves are idiots. There's a reason werewolves are the first shifters that humans name among monsters — often in the same breath as Count Dracula and Frankenstein.

"It makes you think, doesn't it?" Aimee asks, glancing over at the semi in the next lane.

She's still fretting about whether people assume some comic-book feline fatale is a shifter and what that means for the media or society or both. She's like that. We've only known each other for a few months, and she's already dragged me to three political rallies (textbooks, immigration, gay marriage). I don't mind. The women are cute, and snacks are plentiful.

Aimee and I, we're platonic, but she might've been my girl if it weren't for Clyde.

Then again, if Aimee and I had gotten together, I wouldn't be in this what-might-happen place with Kayla. No, that's crazy — the Aimee part, not the Kayla part. It's not like I was madly in love with Aimee. I like her — a lot. She can be flaky and exhausting (in a Goth/New Age/hippie way), but she has this incredible faith in the universe. It's contagious.

You could say I love her as a friend. I do. I love her as a friend. So what's my damage? Aimee was the first girl I cared about as more than booty and, of all the other guys in the world, she chose Clyde Gilbert instead of me. *Clyde. Gilbert.*

What can I say? This Cat man has his pride.

"Bruce Wayne isn't some random society dude with a personality disorder," Clyde insists. "He's the *ultimate* society dude with a personality disorder. There's a difference."

"Tell that to Tony Stark," I reply, hoping I remember right that he's Iron Man.

"You *wish* you were Tony Stark," the Wild Card informs me.

Aimee yawns. We're coming up on Denton, Texas, en route to Jess's aunt's house in Pawhuska, Oklahoma (otherwise known, I've been told, as Osage Nation). We left Pine Ridge not long after midnight, and it's around 4 A.M. now. Werepeople have more endurance than humans. Of course

Cats relish naps and I sure could use one, but Aimee and Jess must be exhausted.

Peso barks, scratching the tops of my thighs — again. It's all I can do not to hiss him into quivering submission, but Kayla would have a fit.

In the rearview mirror, I glimpse flashing lights coming up fast from behind.

"Should I floor it?" Jess asks, and suddenly we're all wide awake.

YOSHI

WE'RE FIVE TEENAGERS, two of whom are naked and cuffed, in a borrowed police vehicle with a small, highly vocal, constantly-in-motion dog. Plus, Kayla is hugely recognizable.

Aimee cranes her neck to look. "I doubt a high-speed chase is the way to go."

I have a mental image of helicopters and live TV. "That would be bad."

Clyde snorts. "What? You don't think we're getting enough media coverage?"

I ask, "Other suggestions?"

"We split up," Kayla begins. "Shifters, jump out. Humans, say we kidnapped you and forced Jess to drive.

Play dumb. Claim you don't know anything, and take Peso home."

At least she agrees that we shouldn't have brought the dog.

"Bad idea." Jess turns down the radio. "Sweetie, this is a police car. The back doors don't open from the inside, and in case you didn't notice, your windows are barred."

Humans tend to underestimate shifter strength. I bet we could kick the doors open, but leverage is an issue. Again, I struggle against the metal binding.

No use, not that I'm down with leaping onto the highway. The fact that shifters heal fast doesn't mean a semi couldn't flatten us for good.

Clyde pitches in. "If the cop makes us get out of the car, we can take him."

"In cuffs?" Kayla asks.

He flashes me a grin and holds the keys up for us to see.

Asshole! Leaning toward the open cage window, I snarl, "You said Aimee lost them!"

Aimee swats the Wild Card. "Not funny. I felt terrible!"

The cop isn't messing around. He's pulled up alongside us. Sensing the heightened tension, Peso starts shaking and drooling. He'd better not throw up.

"Pull over," I say. "Clyde, can you knock out that separator thing?"

"Do not disturb the cage," Jess orders him. "You'll hurt yourself and my dad's car, too." She hits the turn signal.

"Panicking won't solve anything. We don't need to give him another reason to be suspicious, and you can bet he's got a dash cam."

I hadn't thought of that. "You speak cop," I reply. "You take point."

Jess pulls over, muttering, "No pressure."

Grateful I'm the one behind the driver, I angle myself to conceal Kayla as much as possible. I release my fur over my lower half to mimic a pair of pants. A long shot, but it's dark. I've got more control than most shifters, even most Cats. I hope the cop doesn't look too closely. He's getting out on the side of the highway behind us. "Jess, what're we dealing with?"

"Trooper," she replies, glancing at the rearview mirror. "Young guy; his gun's out."

"His gun's out?" Aimee echoes. "Is that normal? That's not normal, is it?"

"Hush," Jess whispers, lowering her window. "Evenin', Officer, is there a problem?"

He's short, stocky in his crisp tan uniform. It's not clear if we, as shifters, have any legal rights. He might shoot us all, not realizing until too late that Jess and Aimee are humans.

I tilt my head, trying to study the cop, not sure what to make of his silence. Then the breeze slips in. I open my mouth to sample it and exhale. "He's a wereperson." That doesn't guarantee he's on our side, but it improves the odds.

"A Tasmanian weredevil," Clyde adds, like species matters at the moment.

"Damn, damn, damn, damn." The weredevil spits and kicks at the gravel. "You're them, aren't you? The Cats everyone's talking about." Glowering, he holsters his gun. "We need to talk. Meet me at the next McDonald's, and don't even think about making a run for it."

AIMEE

THE MOST AMAZING THING about shifters isn't their transformations or their animal-trait superpowers or, at least
with certain species, their radiating sex appeal. All of that
pales next to their appetites. They have sky-high metabo-
lisms, and they eat more meals than hobbits.

Jess and I stroll into the twenty-four-hour McDonald's.
The dining area is nearly deserted except for a husband-
wife trucker team nursing cups of coffee, a guy with a soul
patch plucking at a bass guitar, and a pregnant woman with
a sad face eating apple slices.

After a quick trip to the restrooms, we check out the
menu options. It's Monday. Back in Austin, the morning bell rings at Waterloo High in another five hours.

I somehow doubt I'm going to make it. "We'll take eight Bacon Habanero Ranch Quarter Pounders with large fries." That's two each for the werepeople, including the state trooper. They'd probably be happier with three, but I only have so much cash and I'm not sure how long it has to last. "Plus four vanilla shakes, four apple pies, a bottle of water . . ." I glance at Jess. "How 'bout you?"

"Diet Coke." If she's taken aback by the size of my order, she doesn't show it. "Want to split Chicken McNuggets?"

I do. Addressing the clerk, I add, "We'll also have an order of McNuggets —"

"Oh, and a chocolate cone," Jess puts in, stifling a yawn.

"Make that two." I like her. We met earlier tonight when she appeared out of nowhere at Town Park behind the wheel of our getaway car. Jess is calm, easygoing, with a good sense of humor . . . and human. It's nice for a change, not being the only *Homo sapiens* in the group.

The Cats have settled at a bright yellow metal picnic table alongside the colorful outdoor play area to wait for the state trooper. They're free of the cuffs and wrapped in blankets from the trunk. After a potty break, we left Peso in the backseat with the window cracked.

Clyde is across the street at the mega truck stop, picking up clothes for Yoshi and Kayla.

Male shifters usually shave twice a day, but Cats (their Lion cousins included) tend to be noticeably less hirsute in human form than, say, Wolves or Bears. I hardly ever see the boys this furry. It's amazing how fast they can pass for grown men.

Of course, Yoshi's almost a grown man. He'll graduate high school in six weeks or so, assuming he can yank up his grades. Tonight's drama aside, I'm not worried about him. Yoshi has style and swagger. He uses his lean, muscled swimmer's build to full advantage. He used to be that guy your mom warned you about, but lately he's gravitating toward something real.

"Here goes nothing," Jess muses aloud as we exit carrying plastic trays loaded with food and drinks.

As we approach the table, the cop jogs over from the parking lot, the soles of his polished black combat boots hitting concrete. I envy Jess's light jacket. It's in the mid-sixties, not that the werepeople, who run warmer, seem to notice the cold. Seconds later she tosses a boxed Quarter Pounder at the trooper. It's a gesture that says (human or not) she isn't intimidated.

The stocky weredevil grunts, catching the box. He sniffs before he opens it. We're hoping the beef improves his mood.

By the time I've unscrewed the cap from my water bottle, the shifters have each inhaled half a burger. Yoshi breaks the silence. "What's on your mind, Officer?"

The weredevil turns to gesture with a fry at Kayla. "I'm wondering how you could be so stupid as to get caught on video, and this weekend to boot. Your image is everywhere.

There are already websites selling tote bags and Frisbees with your face on them."

At the risk of stereotyping, this isn't the first Tasmanian weredevil I've met, and they skew cranky. Yoshi, apparently thinking the same thing, laughs. "You don't happen to have a vicious little sister? Eighth-grader named Teghan?"

"Yoshi Kitahara?" The cop is frowning so deeply it looks like his forehead might split.

Yoshi spreads his arms in self-congratulation. "Guilty as charged."

"You got the brat home safe!" The trooper offers his hand across the table. "Call me Oliver." The two shake. The lingering mistrust evaporates. It turns out Oliver is Teghan's cousin. Central Texas werepeople are tightly networked. Everybody seems to know one another within two or three degrees of separation.

This winter Yoshi and Teghan were among werepeople who were captured and brought to a remote tropical island in the South Pacific to be hunted for sport by billionaires — including magic users and the undead. Yoshi not only saw to it that Teghan survived their hunt. He played big brother to her through the whole ordeal, and they catch up now and then over donuts.

I got snatched, too, but since I'm human, my captors decided I'd be more useful as kitchen help, and Clyde was caged — he was on crutches at the time. This was before he discovered that he was half Lion. But afterward he found himself among the hunted as well.

Clyde returns at a brisk pace from his shopping errand and hands Kayla the bag. With his Lossum (Lion + Possum) hearing, he didn't miss any of the exchange.

"She's dead now," Oliver says. "Teghan. Murdered."

Kayla, who retrieved a plain gray T-shirt and black sweatpants from the bag, pauses in her effort to slip them on under the blanket. Clyde sinks onto the yellow metal bench.

Yoshi's the first to respond. "What?" He covers his eyes. "*Who?*"

"Don't know," Oliver replies. "It looked like a professional hit — execution style, which makes no sense. There're a couple of shifters from the Austin Police Department investigating, but it seems like the only case that matters right now is the governor's kidnapping."

"The governor was kidnapped?" I exclaim. "The governor of Texas?"

Oliver glances from one of us to the next. "You haven't heard about the weresnake?"

AIMEE

"I'LL SHOW YOU." Oliver boots his phone, fiddles a moment. With Jess maneuvering the blanket to protect Kayla's modesty, the Cat girl finishes getting dressed. Then they join Yoshi in coming around the table so that they can see.

It's a clip from an Austin TV news station. The screen fills with the Serpent's head. It's a mottled beige color with darker brown triangle patterns flaring from the eyes and two short horns rising from the nose. Orange eyes. I've met weremammals and werebirds, but werereptiles?

Clyde slips his arm around me, and I snuggle in.

"Herpetologists are saying it resembles the Gaboon viper from sub-Saharan Africa," Oliver informs us. "No word yet on whether this *Vipera sapiens* is literally venom-ous, but it might as well be."

The Snake opens its jaws. Assuming its head is roughly on scale with a human's, its fangs are over three inches long. "I am Seth." The voice is raspy, lingering on the *S*.

Believe it or not, that's not the weirdest part. It's that he's talking comfortably as a full-on Snake. A wereperson in animal form has to partly retract the shift to speak at all.

Seth says, "I'm sure you recognize my distinguished guest." The video cuts to show the forty-something gov-ernor. Her light brown curls are a mess, her mascara is smeared, and her red suit is rumpled. She stares into the camera like she's challenging us somehow.

The Snake takes center screen again. "On behalf of shape-shifters everywhere, we have taken the governor of Texas as a declaration of war against the human race. Rest assured there will be no peace until *Homo sapiens* accepts its rightful role as our subordinate."

With a flick of his finger, Oliver shuts his phone down. "Hit the air early this evening, but on the down low, the governor went missing on Friday. People are wigging out. There was talk going around that state and local police would be sent door-to-door, looking to arrest any shifter they could find. A bunch of cops resigned in protest or threatened to." We heard something about that back in Pine Ridge. Now it makes more sense. Oliver adds, "Anyway, the whole operation turned out to be a BS rumor,

25

and it's just a matter of paperwork before everybody's back on the job."

"Is there any proof the Snake isn't acting alone?" Jess wants to know.

"Bear DNA was found in the governor's mansion," Oliver says. "For what that's worth."

"No demands?" Jess asks, her ice cream melting. "No list of grievances?"

"Did I miss something?" Kayla adds. "Did we *elect* a Snake as our spokesperson?"

Yoshi shakes his head and takes a T-shirt out of the bag. It's a V-neck pink women's XL with sparkly angel kittens on front. He pulls it on.

"Hang on," Clyde says. "I thought there was no such thing as a werereptile."

"That would make Seth a Cryptid," I reply. They're apparently more common than I thought. That Pacific island — Daemon Island — that served as the stage for the shifter hunt? It was run by a different kind of Cryptid, members of an intelligent, secretive, largely unknown species. Furry snowpeople devoted to technology (especially air-conditioning) and eco devo, prone to family drama and bad hairstyles, self-described environmentalists, who're fond of eating yak.

Yoshi slams his fist into the center of the metal table, denting it. The noise is too big. We all brace for someone to come running out of the restaurant and scold us. No one does.

"Sorry about that," he says. "I'm okay." He takes a breath. "The symbolism of a weresnake sucks. A lot of humans already believe shifters are demonic. There's that ridiculous story floating around the Internet that the snake in the Garden of Eden was a shape-shifter."

"It's not only on the Internet," Clyde adds. "And it's been floating around since before forever." He picks up his apple pie and addresses Oliver. "How bad is the fallout?"

Oliver draws his gun and looks at it like he's aching to shoot somebody. "The Snake and the governor could be anywhere. The whole state's on lockdown."

"Lockdown?" Kayla asks, stealing the last of Yoshi's fries.

Oliver puts the weapon away. "They're mostly symbolic, but there's a roadblock on every highway heading out of Texas, at the Mexican border, the docks. TSA is on the lookout. Human bigots are nothing new, but the Snake has given regular people a reason to be afraid. And you . . ." He toasts Kayla with his vanilla shake. "You've become the most recognizable shape-shifter in Texas."

The Texas Talker, **April 21**
Op-Ed by Hailey Haluska

The high-profile kidnapping of Governor "Laughin' Linnie" Lawson by a weresnake named Seth may well boost her viability as a potential candidate for the U.S. presidency.

That's assuming, of course, she's rescued alive.

"I have the best job in the world," Lawson was quoted as saying last month. "My heart is here, in the heart of Texas, serving the fine citizens who sent me to the governor's office."

Despite a flurry of recent gaffes, few doubt Lawson will run. Presidential hopefuls often deny plans to seek the nation's highest office until they've fully gauged their resources, weighed the opposition, and can capitalize on an opportune news cycle.

The question has always been: How can she hope to overshadow the dynasties that have dominated presidential politics for the past several administrations? Supporters admired her brass and boots, but outside the state, her reputation dwindled. Or in other words, pundits have asked, why take Laughin' Lawson seriously?

The kidnapping is a game-changer. Although the native Dallasite was elected with a more moderate stance on shape-shifters, she's taken a much harder line in recent weeks.

Lawson has become a household name, an international media sensation in her own right. In the short term, she may come off as a victim, but as the living symbol of threatened humanity, leaders from both major political parties are rallying behind her.

KAYLA

"WE'RE GOING HOME," Yoshi and Clyde both announce. Hearing the other speak the same words at the same time antagonizes them both. On reflex, they glare at each other, and Yoshi hisses. If they were in Cat and Lion form, respectively, they'd be lashing their tails.

Aimee sets her hand on Clyde's wrist, and that ends it. He breaks eye contact first, and then Yoshi preserves his composure by pulling on sweatpants and flip-flops. I reach for the bag to retrieve a pair of flip-flops myself.

When they say "home," they mean Austin. Jess's relatives can't protect us if we can't cross into Oklahoma, and there's no way we're returning to Pine Ridge anytime soon.

"Call it a gut feeling," Oliver says, "but I suggest y'all lose your phones. Get off the grid. Make it harder for anyone to track and make an example out of you."

An eighteen-wheeler pulls up as Aimee's clearing the table. Yoshi and Clyde make a show of assisting her, and Jess's lips curl into a half smile that means she's picked up on the boys' rivalry. I hate that Jess is in the middle of this mess, but her presence is reassuring.

We were best friends. Then, a few years ago, I discovered my Cat heritage and pulled away—at first for her safety (transformations are scary at first) and then because . . . I don't know. Keeping a secret isn't much different from lying, especially when it's the secret of your species, what you really are. It was all pointless. Turns out, she's known I'm a Cat for some time anyway. Now it's headline news. I was just starting to feel comfortable in my Cat skin, to really own it, when the shooting began. Everything's changed so fast. It feels like our whole world is teetering.

"Well, it's been fun." Oliver noisily sucks out the last of his milk shake. "I've got to check in before my dispatcher gets suspicious. And by the way, we never met."

From a distance, my Chihuahua lets loose with a mournful howl.

"Jess," I begin. "I want you to take Peso and go with Oliver."

Jess swallows the last McNugget. "I can't just give y'all my dad's car and —"

"You're too tired to keep driving," Yoshi points out. "Once we hit town, I'll leave it in the Austin Antiques parking lot. He can pick it up there."

"Talk to our folks," I add. "Find out what you can. Report back."

When my parents adopted me from Ethiopia, they had no idea that I was a werecat. But they've always stood firm by my side, and Dad is in deep when it comes to Texas politics. Between him and Sheriff Bigheart, they'll put together the behind-the-scenes scoop.

"I guess I could say you were a runaway," the weredevil muses out loud.

"Pen," Aimee demands, and the cop hands one over. She scribbles a 78704 address on a napkin. "You should be able to find us here," she tells Jess, handing it over. "Or at least whoever's home should be able to point you in our direction."

Aimee has decided where we're going. Never mind that she's a petite human or that with her turquoise-striped blond hair, tats, and piercings, she looks like a cute Goth elf. The boys defer to her, and, under the circumstances, I'm glad they've got someone in common.

In the parking lot, I give Jess a hug. "A thousand times, thank you."

She whispers in my ear. "Sweetie, how well do you know these people?"

How well is debatable. How long? It's early Monday morning. I first met Yoshi on Friday night and Aimee, then Clyde, after that. I appreciate Jess looking out for me. She doesn't seem worried about leaving with Oliver, but he's a cop and she's been raised around law enforcement. "They were there for me in Pine Ridge," I say. "They're here for me now."

Everyone's waiting. I gather Peso in my arms and kiss his forehead, whispering, "Hey, little guy. Be good for Jess." He'll be safer, but I hate letting him go. My parents treasure me. But to Peso, I'm his whole world. Well, me, food, and squeaky toys.

A moment later I can still hear him whimpering in the other car. Fortunately, Yoshi doesn't hesitate to pull out of the McDonald's lot. As we pass the sign pointing to I-35 South, I ask, "What now? Besides Austin, I mean. What happens when we get there?"

I'm not good at lying low. I don't like it, and I really have to pee.

"It's not obvious?" Clyde asks, taking Aimee's hand. "We're going to rescue the governor from the weresnake. We're going to prove that all shifters aren't black hats, and we're going to get the feds to back the hell off our collective ass. We'll strategize from there."

"And we're going to find out who killed Teghan," Yoshi puts in.

CLYDE

WE'RE AT A REST AREA a couple of miles south of Salado. It's about an hour north of Austin, with traffic. Yoshi and Kayla are in the restrooms. She's too much of a lady to squat by the road.

The sun's up. I'm primed to get home and get on with it. We've taken our hits, but we're full-fledged heroes now. We've defeated dark forces and arctic asshats and even put Kayla's ex-boyfriend's preppy soul to rest. The feds took us by surprise in Pine Ridge. But we're not losing to a bunch of trigger-happy humans or a fugly werereptile with attitude.

Besides, for the first time in days, I've got Aimee all to myself.

It took us a while to get here, relationship-wise. She almost clicked with my buddy Travis and then crushed on Yoshi. I was shocked when we got home from Daemon Island and she picked me over the Cat man. But it's working. Us, that is. She's my paintball buddy, the other half of our dynamic dishwashing duo. She can debate the differences between Bruce Wayne, Tony Stark, and Oliver Queen for hours.

Staring through the barred back window, Aimee yawns. "You know, I bet there are security cameras here."

Probably. On the other hand, we've pulled over twice for fuel, and gas stations have surveillance systems, too. I loop my arms around her waist. There's a limit to how paranoid we can be and still manage to function.

"It's a state rest stop," I say, trying to reassure her. "Oliver says that we're not technically wanted for anything." Granted, that didn't stop the feds from shooting at us — or at least at the Cats — earlier. "Besides, it's too late now."

Aimee fumbles for the pointless door latch. "What if something happens? We'll be helpless, trapped in here. What's taking them so long?"

I can't resist. "Yoshi's taking a dump."

Aimee gently elbows me. I can hear the smile in her voice. "He is not."

The pristine facility is designed to resemble a grist mill. We're the only vehicle in the lot. The American flag flutters in the light wind. There's no sign of the Cats coming out of the front entrance. Not yet. I pull Aimee closer and press a kiss against the crosses tattooed around her neck. "Sure he is. He let loose a couple of silent farts, getting out of the car."

"You're horrible!" she replies, laughing. "You're crude and gross and unromantic —"

"And you love me," I whisper.

Aimee goes silent. I didn't mean to get so serious. Or at least I didn't mean for her to take it that way. Not in the backseat of this ungodly uncomfortable cop car that stinks like vomit (not that her human nose can tell) in a parking lot off I-35. We goof off all the time, but she knows it's real for me. I know it's real for her, too. But we've never said the L-word like that.

She slips her small hands over mine. "I do," Aimee assures me. "I love you. Even when you're . . . crude and gross and unromantic and snacking on crickets . . ."

"I hardly ever do that anymore." It's a habit from my Possum-only days.

She laughs. "You try kissing someone with bug breath."

"Hey," Kayla begins, opening the front passenger-side door. "I brought you both waters."

"Thanks." Aimee accepts the chilled plastic bottles through the window in the cage. The Cats may not recognize the disappointment in Aimee's voice, but I do.

I can't leave Aimee hanging. I have to tell her that I love her, too.

CLYDE

"YO!" I lead Kayla and Yoshi through my front door. Aimee's apartment isn't far from here. We dropped her off a few minutes ago. "Mom? Dad? Babies?"

No answer. The pacifier on the floor isn't unusual. Neither is the stuffed toy possum that's been tossed on the couch or the rattle dangling off the coffee table.

Dad's schoolwork is missing from the kitchen (he's studying to get certified as a science teacher). The coffeemaker is cool to the touch. Dad's an early riser, usually up by 6 A.M. It's going on 9 A.M. now. Morning rush hour slowed us up getting into town.

The refrigerator art catches my eye. A mishmash of baby handprints in four different colors. I remember Mom sitting the plump kits (Clara, Cleatus, Claudette, and Clint) on an old bedsheet around the butcher paper. "Messy," she admitted, "but look how happy they are."

"That scent," Kayla begins. "It's —"

"Werebear," Yoshi finishes. "It's fresh. I detect *Homo sapiens*, too."

Nobody I recognize. Werebears are the strongest shifters on land. They can scent out fellow werepeople faster than Wolves. The males look like NFL linebackers. Ditto for most of the females. Cutting across the family room, I check the bathroom off the hall, my parents' room. Their bed isn't made. Mom's purse is gone. No diaper bag in the nursery. My leopard gecko isn't in my room either. His tank is missing. Where's my family?

I think of Lula, Teghan. I wander back down the hall. "What if they're dead?"

"Don't be paranoid." Kayla meets me halfway. "Where do y'all store the luggage?"

At least Yoshi had the sense to wait in the family room. I fling open the master bedroom closet. The luggage is gone. "Why would they take Jara Hamee?"

Trailing after me, Kayla asks, *"Who?"*

"My gecko." Along with the stink of diapers and my mom's spicy perfume, I detect anxiety. My parents packed up the kits and took Jara Hamee with them because they weren't sure when any of us would be coming back.

I reach for my phone. I scroll to the text from my

mom: Don't come home. FHPU is looking for you. We're in Amarillo. Stay away from AB.

Amarillo. They must've gone to Aunt Jenny and Uncle Victor's. There's nothing about my meeting them there. If the FHPU came here, I don't blame them for taking off. Especially with the quads to think about. On average, shifter parents aren't less protective than humans. But they don't go full barrel as long. By the time we're in high school, it's expected that we start to look after ourselves. But stay away from AB? Aimee Barnard? Why?

"I'm going to grab a few things," I mutter. "Then we should move out."

I duck into my bedroom to shove clothes into my old backpack.

"Don't forget your razor," Kayla says.

When I rejoin the Cats in the family room, they're watching the TV news. There's a sketch of an arctic asshat — yeti, snowman, Sasquatch — whatever you want to call them. They call themselves *Homo deific*. It means "God people." As if.

They walk upright. They've got heavy jaws, ape-long arms, and bulky torsos. They're not shifters. They're not humans either, but they are mono forms. They can't shape-shift. They're more closely related to *Homo sapiens* than werepeople.

It was their kind that kidnapped us (minus Kayla)

to Daemon Island. Where I was caged like an animal. Where Aimee became a house slave. One of them reported us to the FHPU. He video recorded Kayla shifting and sent the footage to the media. After pretending to be our friend.

International News Network

Transcript: April 21

Anchor: Breaking news! Both the modern remains and a 2,000-year-old set of remains from the same newly discovered species have gone missing. It's been speculated that they might prove the existence of wereapes or a primitive species of man. Possibly even the Missing Link.

Reports that the contemporary creature showed signs of modern dentistry and a neural implant have fueled speculation of human-level intelligence.

Last night the historic specimen, originally found in Kazakhstan, was reported stolen from the University of New Mexico, and the modern one, found off the coast of Costa Rica, likewise disappeared en route to UNM.

In the past week, this so-called "Cryptid species" has set the scientific world ablaze. We're live with Dr. Uma Urbaniak, the UNM professor of prehistoric anthropology credited with finding the fossilized remains.

Dr. Urbaniak, is it true that a jury of experts was en route to join you in Albuquerque to examine, compare, and verify the authenticity of both sets of remains?

Dr. Urbaniak: "Jury" may be overstated, but yes, a few of my colleagues had planned to visit.

AIMEE

WHEN MY FRIENDS DROPPED ME OFF, Clyde gave me a Hollywood kiss good-bye. It made me feel better about what he didn't say in the car. I'm trying not to overreact. We were interrupted, and Clyde's been through a lot. Only a few months ago, he was talking big about graduating from sidekick to hero.

We're sophomores, a couple years younger than most of our friends, and this was back when he thought he was exclusively *Homo marsupial.* He even glued dominoes made from shifter bones all over his SUV and nicknamed it "the Bone Chiller."

Then, after Daemon Island, he was a changed man. Clyde's as hunky as Yoshi, though he doesn't own it the

Anchor: Today supermodel Saffron Flynn said—quote—"I think it's a hoax. Like Bigfoot. This professor lady is probably looking for attention or money or whatever." Now that the specimens have disappeared, can you prove her wrong?

Dr. Urbaniak: I am not in the habit of responding to criticism by supermodels.

same way. My Lossum is broader through the shoulders, with silver-flecked, thick golden hair. More solid than slinky, he's shot up this past year, filled out. His features have lost that pinched look he had when he was younger. It's not all superficial. He also yanked up his grades and donated his "super" car to the interfaith coalition (a shifter-friendly organization of demon busters). Only problem? His Possum mom has been closemouthed about his biological Lion father. It's been tough for Clyde to process — the paternity issue, being of dual species. Worse because of the secrecy.

When I walk in the front door, Mom puts down her pink highlighter. "Where have you been?" she begins. "I just hung up with Sergio at Sanguini's. I was about to call the police. You're supposed to be at school. Don't you have a quiz today in English?"

Mom is set up on the sofa, using a foldout TV tray as a desk. She's been trying to reinvent herself from retail sales to life coach. The titles stacked beside her include *Coaching Yourself to Coach Others, 9 Secrets to Enduring Success,* and my personal favorite: *Embracing Your Inner Yoda.* Next to all that is a copy of the *Capital City News.* I glimpse the banner headline — MONSTERS AMONG US? — above a grainy image of Kayla in mostly human form, but with pointed ears and long tail, next to a better-quality image of the weresnake Seth.

"I left you three voice messages and sent a dozen texts,"

Mom goes on. "You can't keep disappearing like this. I know it's been hard, the way things have been with your father, and I understand that teenagers test limits. That's healthy and normal. I don't want to squash your emerging woman power, but —"

"I . . ." I want to protest that I don't *keep* disappearing. But I did go to Michigan. That was the road trip that landed Clyde in a coma, and I was kidnapped — though it's not like I planned it — to Daemon Island.

On the wicker coffee table, Mom's burning Tibetan sandalwood incense to calm her nerves. I rub my eyelids and cross to our toffee-colored Rowling leather armchair (her Pottery Barn employee discount at work). "I can explain, but could you answer a couple of questions for me first?" Before she can protest, I add, "About Dad. What's going on with him?"

That shuts down her momentum. "Okay . . . He's been promoted to VP of MCC Enterprises, so he's moving back to Texas. It should be any day now." Dad's been working as the lead PR guy for MCC Implants (a subsidiary) in Hong Kong. "What do you mean, 'What's going on with him?'"

We used to be so close, me and Dad. Before my parents fell apart, Mom used to joke that she was "the other woman" in the relationship. And then . . . It was like he forgot about us. We were an expensive nuisance from a life he'd left behind.

But things have been better recently. He's caught up on his child-support payments. He gave Mom a spa gift certificate for her birthday. I don't have high hopes that they'll get back together, but my life would be easier if they were friends.

"This weekend I caught him on the TV news," I say. "Did you know that MCC is making brain chips that can track and control werepeople? What with the kidnapping of the governor, the werecat video out of Pine Ridge, the death of that little girl . . ."

"Jacinda Finch," she prompts. It's been all over the news as a "weretiger attack." Finch was only four years old and the daughter of an Internet mogul from New York.

I pick my words carefully. "All of that is great for Dad's company. The more frightened humans are of werepeople, the easier it is for MCC to market and sell the implants."

Mom flicks at glance at the newspaper. "You know that your father and I disagree when it comes to werepeople."

Yes, I know. He thinks they're monsters. She thinks they're beloved children of Mother Earth. It's romantic, my mom's attitude. Clyde finds it at times funny, at times condescending. "The brain chip," I continue. "Has Dad talked to you about it? Do you know how close it is to hitting the market? Did he mention—?"

"What does any of this have to do with—?"

"I'm sorry I lied to you." My mother may be flaky, but she isn't stupid. "I was in Pine Ridge." I reach for the newspaper beside her. "At the Founders' Day weekend festival." I hold up the front page. "With my furry friends."

"I figured as much," she replies, and I'm the one who's surprised. "Your father called yesterday. He says he needs to talk to you in person. In the meantime, he's demanding that you quit your job and sever all ties with Yoshi and Clyde."

YOSHI

I LEFT KAYLA AND CLYDE in the car. Grams isn't exactly a people person. Or even a werepeople person. But she *might* lend me her pickup, and I promised Jess I'd leave the sheriff's car in this lot.

It's quiet outside. Sunny, as usual. Few parked cars on this end of the shopping center. No sign of Grams's truck. At this time of day, Donna's Diner is the only draw. I could really go for a platter of fried chicken over waffles. (McDonald's was nearly six hours ago.) The liquor store, the consignment boutique, the cupcake shop . . . nothing else opens for twenty minutes. Neither does Austin Antiques, owned by my grandmother. But it's close enough to 10 A.M. that Grams should be brewing the purple acai green tea that's offered, along with miso soup, to shoppers on a complimentary basis.

I was babysitting the antiques mall when I unexpectedly went AWOL to Pine Ridge. I don't have my keys, the walls are beige-colored brick, and the back door is made of reinforced steel. I risk Grams's wrath by breaking the lock in front. The alarm that should go off doesn't.

Against the front wall, Grams's prize bonsai collection sits pretty beneath the gold-framed beveled mirrors. Parallel to that, the polished gold pocket watches gleam next to white lace gloves and cameo brooches in the glass counter beneath the cash register. The ceiling is popcorn and the overheads are cheap fluorescent, but Grams does her best to class up the place. I don't hear boiling water or smell fresh tea. My instincts are screaming that something's wrong.

Bam. The first gunshot rings out, and in one smooth motion, I flatten my body to the cracked manila-colored tile floor. A familiar voice shouts, "You damn fool!"

Bam. I swivel my body into the first row of dealer booths and crawl behind the 1950s jukebox. "Grams! It's me, Yoshi!"

There's no telling whether that'll help or hurt my situation. Since she moved to Austin, Grams and I have come to a strained peace. She must've taken care of me as a baby — bathed me, changed my diapers, held my hands as I learned to walk. But mostly, growing up, Ruby and I fended for

50

ourselves. Grams smacked us — sometimes claws in, sometimes claws out — whenever the mood struck her. Back in Kansas, she chased me off the family farm — at gunpoint — for a literal roll in the hay in our barn with a girl whose name I don't remember. *Bam.*

She's a tough old puss. She used to run a safe house for shifters on the run. Truth is, she's always been a bit trigger-happy.

"Grams, *come on!*" I yell, backing into a brass hat rack. "I didn't abandon the mall. I accidentally touched a cursed antique — a cat-shaped carousel figure — and teleported to Pine Ridge." *Bam.*

"I met a friend of yours there," I continue. *Bam.* "Zelda. A carny Cat fortune-teller engaged to some guy she calls 'the Old Alligator Man.'"

The building goes blessedly silent.

"Zelda's getting hitched?" Grams mutters from approximately row five, booth seven.

Based on the angle of the shots, I'm betting she's tucked into a squat on top of the life-size bronze longhorn statue (retails for three grand).

"Everybody's getting married except me." Raising her voice, she adds, "Yoshi, what dumbass thing did you do to set the feds on yourself and your sister?"

My sister? "Is Ruby all right?"

A sudden crash is followed by more clanking ones and shattering glass. I slip from my hiding place and leap,

51

wobbling on my toes, to the top of the nearest booth wall. "Stop!"

Grams springs out of a tight roll to face Kayla, both of them in partial shift — human form but fur covered, saber teeth barred. Grams growls, "Stupid girl."

When the longhorn statue fell, it shattered floor tiles and took down two booths to the left, spilling Magnum P.I. and Power Rangers lunch boxes, Princess Diana memorial plates, and vintage rhinestone hair bobs into the aisle. The Depression glass bottles and pitchers broke into multicolored pieces, dulled by the flickering fluorescent lighting. Our truck-stop flip-flops have flimsy plastic soles. I warn Kayla, "Watch your step!"

Fortunately, Grams's double-barrel shotgun was knocked out of her hands, which in no way means she and my potential girlfriend won't shred each other to dripping scraps of tissue. Even the most serene werepredators have our feral moments, and Grams is far from Zen.

"I am *not* stupid," Kayla replies, as they circle each other.

Where's Clyde? "She's not stupid, Grams," I say, jumping down. "That's Kayla Morgan. A nice small-town were-cat girl with perfect grades from a respectable family, and I like her." I make my way over to stand between them. "In a capital *R*, relationship kind of way."

"You do?" Grams and Kayla both exclaim, straightening.

At least the fight's over. Grams's surprise is that I care about a girl. Kayla's . . . well, it's not like I haven't been flirting with her since we met, but she's been haunted — literally — by an ex-boyfriend, and she picked up on my mixed feelings for Aimee. The way I see it, it's time we both moved on. To each other.

"Smart, eh?" Grams asks. "How smart?"

"Academic scholarship to Cal Tech," Kayla snaps back. "Engineering." What with events of the past twenty-four hours, that's probably shot to hell. I feel guilty now for envying that she *had* a future, one more satisfying than hocking antiques under Grams's thumb.

Grams nods slowly, gestures to me. "What do *you* see in *him*?"

Of course. Then again, I do look like an idiot in this sparkly angel kittens T-shirt. Or at least I look like a five-year-old girl. I should've grabbed one of Clyde's shirts when we were at his place, but I didn't want to give him the satisfaction. "What's this about Ruby?"

"She eloped!" Grams informs me. "Left with Little Miss Erika Saturday night on the plane for Vermont, said she'd been trying to call you all day. They're still there."

"Ruby's *married?*" My big sis has been seeing Erika only since February, but they're sweet together, which is saying something for my sister, who's training to be a cop and is almost as much of a badass as Grams. Ruby and Erika met cute at Carnaval Brasileiro. On Valentine's Day, they got matching Hello Kitty tattoos on their right butt cheeks. I tagged along with them to South by Southwest, and by then Erika already felt like family. No surprise that Ruby couldn't get ahold of me. I drowned my phone in the river earlier that afternoon. "About the feds . . ."

"They came looking for *both* of you yesterday," Grams explains. "Why?"

"I don't know," I say, honestly baffled.

Grams wrinkles her nose at the smell of the truth. "The newlyweds were planning to come home Monday. I warned Ruby to be on the lookout and told her, what with the weresnake mess, no shifter can pass in or out of Texas right now without being questioned. Knowing your sister, she'd get cheeky with a TSA agent, and they've got zero sense of humor. The way I see it, there's always some damn thing going wrong in the world. They may as well stay put and enjoy their honeymoon."

Clyde moseys up the aisle, sipping from a bowl of miso soup.

"Where the hell have you been?" I want to know.

He shrugs. "What? It wasn't an emergency."

I swear to God. "I was being shot at."

The Wild Card's grin is smug. "Like I said."

Grams scowls at him. "Fetch a broom, boy, and then sweep up that mess of glass. Supply closet is by the restrooms." He doesn't argue, which proves he's not a total idiot.

Kayla, who hasn't met my eyes since my declaration of like, helps Grams lift the bronze longhorn statue back into place. Grams asks, "The FHPU — you know them?"

"We've met," Kayla puts in. "Back in my hometown."

Grams's pupils dilate. She moves closer to Kayla, studying her face, and I begin picking up crap from the floor, trying to look less worried. In the old days, being caught mid-shift by humans might be punishable by banishment, sometimes death, at the claws of your own kind, assuming of course that the *Homo sapiens* in question didn't skin you first. In the info age, the stakes are higher. True, we've got more allies. We're softer with our own — usually. However, Grams is something of a traditionalist.

Toe-to-toe, Kayla's younger, in better physical condition, but Mayor and Mrs. Morgan's princess is no trained fighter. Grams is mean as hell, a retired professional spy (or something like it), and a little mentally unstable.

Grams rests a hand on Kayla's shoulder. It looks reassuring, but she could be bracing my would-be girlfriend to hollow her throat out. Instead, her voice is gentle. "How did it happen?"

Creepy, the way she's being so nice. Trying to play it cool, I set the Bionic Woman lunch box on a plywood shelf and bend to snag a Snoopy one.

Conventional wisdom is that shifters make up less than one percent of the U.S. population and that we confine ourselves to low-income urban and remote areas, that we're mostly vegetarians like weredeer or mountain weregoats. I don't know our real numbers. It's not like there's a shifter box on the census. But we're more plentiful than that, and Cats, Wolves, Bears, and Orcas are by no means endangered species.

Kayla raises her chin, and I'm relieved that she's picked up something about dominance from me and Clyde. "At that hour, with the stormy weather, nobody should've been at the park."

Grams's nod is punctual. Texans can't cope with rain, though they're always praying for it.

"It's secluded, along the riverfront, separated by downtown from residential housing and by a steep, heavily wooded hill from the business district. I wasn't expecting . . ." Kayla takes a breath. "We were performing a ritual to reassemble a fragmented soul, my ex-boyfriend Ben's, so he could move on and also to release the werepeople he was partially possessing, including Yoshi. Someone we trusted secretly filmed me, uploaded the file . . ."

I blow off the Dukes of Hazzard box. "Kayla didn't mean —"

"No, she didn't mean a blasted thing." Grams scoops up a vintage marcasite hairpin and asks me, "Since when are you in the soul-saving business? Or interesting enough to get possessed? And what 'friend' betrayed her?"

I get why Grams is confused. Before meeting Aimee this winter, I was a slacker, a carefree Tom Cat. Grams's knowledge of Daemon Island is sketchy, and she's still putting together what happened in Pine Ridge. "It was a goddamn greedy yeti," I declare. "Junior, that's what he calls himself. He's just a kid — thirteen or so — and your buddy Zelda raised him, so we thought he could be trusted." I don't know what happened to him after that. He could've lumbered back through the forest to Zelda's log cabin on the lake. I can't imagine he'd abandon his house cat, Blizzard. I don't really care. Well, I care about Blizzard. I'm a cat person, after all.

I find a blue glass bottle that survived its fall and set it on top of a nearby cast-iron and wooden school desk. I might have a world history paper due today. I can't remember for sure.

"Howdy," greets a masculine voice from the front of the store. "You open?"

"Uh . . . Ms. Kitahara!" Clyde calls. "Customer!"

"On my way!" Grams lets go of Kayla and whispers, "I'll keep whoever that is busy. Meanwhile, you two clean up this mess — fast — take your dim-witted friend, and get out of here."

Carrying a broom, Clyde turns into the aisle. "The customer's looking for a hunk of shag carpeting that used to be in Graceland."

"Easy mark," Grams mutters. "Listen, kids, the feds are looking for you. Don't go home. Don't go to school. It's not just guns you've got to worry about. They're using Bears for muscle. The working theory is that they're being controlled by neural implant technology."

MCC Implants, I bet. I refuse to get psyched out. Bears may be strong, but they aren't fast. They're even money racing a wereboar or pygmy wereelephant, but Ostriches, Hyenas, Deer . . . any of us Cats are faster. Kayla could blow past a werebear.

KAYLA

I'VE SEEN THE BUMPER STICKERS: **KEEP AUSTIN WEIRD.**
The city boasts hippies and hipsters, bubbas and techies,
gurus and politicos, musicians and movie stars. I've heard
it called "the pretty girl capital of the world." Dad jokes
that it's the Sodom and Gomorrah of Texas. Passing a
bike-riding man in only thong underwear, I'm inclined to
believe him.

Yoshi turns at the large rotating purple metal sculpture
of a bat.

We left Sheriff Bigheart's car near the liquor store and
hot-wired Yoshi's grandmother's truck, which had been
parked behind the diner.

From there we cruised across town to pick up Aimee outside her apartment. Now all four of us are jammed in together, and my outer thigh is pressed tight against Yoshi's.

Do Cat families normally behave like Yoshi and his grams? I have no idea. I didn't even know another wereperson until a week ago. There were the Stubblefield sisters — werecats who owned the antique shop back home on Main — but what with their vanilla rose perfume, I never realized they weren't human. Lula's dead now, gunned down by the FHPU.

Clyde says, "Yoshi's grandmother told us the FHPU is using Bears controlled with implants. How can your dad justify —?"

"There's an argument that using brain chips on werepeople felons is more humane than the death penalty," Aimee says at the stoplight.

That's the kindest face she could put on it, but even states that don't execute humans have no such reservations about werepeople. Our legal rights are slippery. The difference between an accused shifter and a convicted shifter is, well, there isn't one.

The South Congress strip is bursting with nightclubs, restaurants, lodging, bohemian and chic boutiques. There's a 1950s rehabbed motel with a key-shaped neon sign, a burger joint that used to be a gas station, and a costume shop called All the World's a Stage.

"Implants could facilitate a slave class, prostitution." I

shudder. "Breeding for hides . . . It doesn't take much to imagine the applications of MCC's —"

"The company's also involved in medical research," Aimee adds, twisting a pink gemstone ring around her finger. "If your healing abilities could somehow be shared with humans, it could end suffering. Save lives."

The quiet that follows her halfhearted defense becomes painful. Aimee may be in the majority of the general population, but she's in the minority of her social group. "I'm sorry," she gushes. "I can't believe my own father —"

"Not your fault." Yoshi turns down a Screaming Head Colds song on the radio. "I've never even met my parents." His smile is wry. "Or at least I don't remember my mother."

He *likes* me. He said so to his lunatic grandmother with me standing right there. Not that I didn't suspect it earlier. Still, it's something to hear it out loud. Other than our Cat heritage, we've got little in common. I'm tight with my loving parents, and his grams is downright dangerous. I've been raised like a human, where he revels in his inner animal. My roots run deep in Pine Ridge, while he's a new arrival to Austin. I'm competitive-college-bound (or at least I'm supposed to be), and from what I've gathered he's . . . an academic underachiever.

Yoshi's known — and I mean *known* — his share of girls (I can tell), and I've had only the one disastrous relationship. Speaking of which, I spent half of last night exorcising my late ex-boyfriend Ben's fractured spirit. I spent the other half on the run from federal agents and (apparently) werebears . . . so of course I'm obsessing over Yoshi.

It's mental self-preservation. I'm so maxed out by what matters that the trivial is taking over my brain, giving me something less overwhelming to think about. Yeah, that's it.

Regardless, part of me wishes that Clyde had been the one to reassure Aimee about her father instead. I've met other kids of political parents at party fund-raisers. It sucks when your mom or dad makes a gaffe or is down in the polls or, worse, indicted. Graham Barnard's in business, not politics, but he's the company spokesperson, which makes him very public.

Yoshi turns at a boots and Western wear shop, then again into the alley behind it.

"I've never met my dad either, whoever he is," Clyde tells me. "My biological father, I mean. Not my *dad* dad."

I understand. To me, my adoptive parents are my parents, and that's that. Sometimes I think about my birth family, though — more so since I discovered I'm a Cat. Do they wonder about me? Are they even still alive? Beyond Ethiopia, it's a blank. Until the past few days, I've mostly had to piece together what being a Cat means on my own.

I suspect Clyde feels the same way about his inner Lion.

KAYLA

I'M SURPRISED TO DISCOVER that our destination—Sanguini's: A Very Rare Restaurant—is a nondescript one-story brick building with no windows. Clyde proudly informs me that the red neon sign is new. I was expecting . . . more. With its history of murder, jaw-dropping fashions, and a celebrity chef, Sanguini's is infamous.

We park in a newly extended asphalt lot, behind a meticulously labeled vegetable and herb garden. The centerpiece is a six-foot-tall marble statue of an angel—a twentysomething-looking male with flowing hair — depicted on a pedestal in low-riding, form-fitting jeans and a T-shirt that reads COEXIST in the symbols of various religions.

He's my-oh-my sexy, gasp-and-sweat sexy.

The way I was raised, it's bordering on sacrilegious.

Aimee laughs at my expression. "Think of it as an affectionate tribute."

We're buzzed in at the back door, and I take note of the security cameras.

Inside, my Cat ears pick up muffled voices cussing over Tejano music blasting from a radio in the commercial kitchen. My nose detects garlic, oregano, onions. Down the hall, I hear a man with a slight Mexican accent inside an office marked MANAGER.

We pass a handwritten sign that reads *Executive Staff Meeting, Private Party Room* on a door labeled EMPLOYEES ONLY. At that, Aimee and Clyde take off jogging and disappear between red drapes at the end of the hallway. Yoshi mutters, "Executive? I thought they were dishwashers." He ducks into the men's restroom, and I linger in the hallway to wait.

I appreciate having a moment. I'm an only child. For some years I've kept mostly to myself. I'm not used to so much togetherness.

I can hear Yoshi in there, splashing his face. He's incredibly composed for someone who was shot at less than an hour ago. I never figured him for an abused kid. I doubt he thinks of himself that way. But his grams isn't just a big personality. She's damaged somehow.

Once he's back, he offers me his arm and I take it. We grandly pass through the heavy drapes into a schmaltzy dining room — crystal chandeliers, black leather seating, cozy dance floor. Minus the bar area, the place probably sits about fifty. We pick up our pace at the sound of voices arguing. I recognize Clyde's. He's saying, "I'm not going to cower while —"

"Hon, it's been a doozy of a week," Chef Nora says as we reach the entry to the private dining room. She's on the other side of a table set with plates and platters, stacked high with aluminum-foil wraps. The private dining room seats a dozen and, with its faux-painted castle walls and candle-like wall sconces, reflects the restaurant's signature decor.

I met Nora and Freddy, who's also present, earlier this weekend. Nora's one of those older southern ladies who own their curves and rule their kitchens. Freddy's a trim fashionisto in his early forties who runs the catering department. She says, "Those FHPU brutes hurt our Kieren."

I've never met Kieren Morales, but I've heard of him. He's Clyde's closest friend, a Wolf studies scholar who was wrong about the existence of weresnakes. According to

Aimee, he doesn't like Yoshi because the Cat "ogled" some-body. I'm guessing Kieren's girlfriend.

"Kieren!" Aimee exclaims, sinking into a chair. "What happened? When?"

"This morning." Cleaning his wire-framed glasses with a red napkin, Freddy reports, "Meara was in Buda, having just delivered wereraccoon triplets. Roberto had already dropped off Meghan at preschool and gone to teach a class at UT. That left Kieren home alone."

Kieren's mother, Meara Morales, must be a healer. Werepeople don't go to human doctors or hospitals. I had to get creative on my physical examination forms for track and cross-country. Before realizing I was a Cat, my mom took me in for immunizations, eye and hearing checks, but, fortunately, I was never outed with a blood or urine test.

Running a hand through his thick hair, Clyde looks stunned. "How bad is —?"

"Both of his arms are broken," reports a stunning freckled redhead, perched on the edge of the table at the front of the room. "Both shoulders separated, most of his ribs cracked or broken. He has a concussion and spinal compression fractures, so right now shifting is too dangerous. He'll have to heal in human form for a while." She raises her UT sports bottle, and I notice her hand is badly scarred. "The FHPU came looking for you, Clyde," she adds, meeting his gaze. "Their pet werebears roughed him up, trying to get information. He managed to break out through the back door and lost them in the neighborhood."

Freddy motions us in. "Thank God they didn't shoot him."

Clyde says, "Quincie, when can I —?"

"As soon as he's up to it," she replies. "His mama is with him. He's resting now." Her voice has an eerie calmness to it that's pricking at my instincts.

Yoshi and I stay where we are, in the doorway.

"At least Meghan wasn't there," Aimee says, as ever grasping at the bright side. Glancing at me, she adds, "Kayla, this is Quincie P. Morris, the owner of this esteemed establishment. Quincie, meet our newest best friend, Kayla Morgan."

I raise my hand in a halfhearted wave, and her responding nod is almost dismissive. I get the distinct impression that Nora and Freddy have already filled her in on me.

I'm oddly fascinated by this Quincie girl. She's toying with a turquoise-and-silver cross necklace. Crucifix? I write off her rudeness to emotional overload. No hint of shifter to her scent. She's dressed in faded overalls over a T-shirt and red-wine cowboy boots. Yet she exudes "predator" and holds herself like Sanguini's is her territory.

It makes no sense in the face of an unarmed teenage

human girl, but my inner Cat is screaming at me to run fast, run far, and climb the tallest tree I can find.

Yoshi steps into the room at the mention of the death of his young weredevil friend Teghan.

"Paxton didn't survive his visit either," Freddy puts in.

That name is new to me. With this Paxton, I don't detect the kind of grief surrounding Teghan's death or the outrage over Kieren's injuries.

"Teghan and Paxton were on Daemon Island," Yoshi says, mostly for my benefit. "He was dealing transformeaze to werepeople at an underground club downtown and working for the yetis to capture shifters for the hunts. But he did help us escape."

"Thanks to Aimee," Clyde adds, and she brightens at the praise.

"We already called Mei and James to warn them," Chef Nora says. "And Brenek in Chicago, but we can't find Noelle." More island shifters, I assume.

Yoshi relates that the FHPU went to his grams's antique store, searching for him and Ruby. He mentions that his sister is out of state on her honeymoon, and everyone's delighted by that news. Then Clyde reports that his parents packed up "the kits" and his gecko and left town after an FHPU visit, too. What's happening inside feels a lot like family business. Quincie keeps glancing my way like she's not convinced they should be talking so freely in my presence.

Screw that. I may be a total stranger to the redhead and she may rule this restaurant. But it's my name and image that have gone viral, my species that's been outed, and my longtime neighbor Lula who was gunned down in cold blood in my hometown park.

Besides, I earned my bright, shiny future. I want it back.

KAYLA

"WHAT ARE OUR ASSETS?" I ask, inserting myself in the conversation.

Freddy rubs his forehead. "If you mean money—"

"Manpower." I reach for an egg-sausage-cheddar burrito. I'll say this for restaurant folk: They're not going to let me starve. "Make that werepeople power. Allies, muscle, special skills."

The room quiets. I'm not sure if it's because I asked the wrong question or the right one. Freddy winks at Nora. They seem endearingly charmed, but nobody's in a hurry to answer.

"Kayla," Freddy begins, once I wipe salsa from my mouth. "Stand for a moment." I don't see a reason not to until he pulls a cloth measuring tape from his shirt pocket and begins to unwind it. "We've been expecting you." Freddy wraps the tape around my back, bust level.

Sweet baby Jesus! What's he doing? Raising my hands, I say, "Excuse me?"

"Sizing in the junior's category — or any category — is inconsistent," he explains. "If you're going to be out and about, we can't have you looking like the girl who's been all over the news. It won't take much. Clothes, hair, makeup — maybe a few piercings or a tattoo . . ."

"I am not defiling my body with ink!" I exclaim. Aimee blinks at me, Clyde smirks, and I remember the matching half-inch-tall crosses tattooed around their necks. Aimee has tiny skulls on her ankles, too. "Nothing personal."

Freddy pockets the tape. "Runner's build. I'll pick up a mix of outfits and accessories — stealth ensembles, everyday wear, and red carpet. Shoe size? Bra?"

I resist the impulse to cross my arms over my chest. "A bit personal, don't you think?"

Freddy catches himself up short. "Sorry, heat of the moment. I —"

"*Tsk.*" Chef Nora hands me a pen and a white napkin from the Tia Leticia's takeout bag. "Write it all down here." She adds, "Freddy used to be a la-di-da event planner in Chicago. He's done his share of styling young . . . and youthful-looking ladies and gentlemen."

"Youthful-looking" is apparently a joke that Yoshi and

I aren't in on, but everybody else in the room is mildly amused. I'm getting better using my instincts to gauge emotion, now that I've learned it's something shifters excel at and not just my imagination on overdrive.

Freddy is middle-aged and definitely gay (back in Pine Ridge, he mentioned a boyfriend). It's not like he cares about my bust and booty for any reason beyond wardrobe. What's more, his designer clothes are tailored, his fingernails buffed — my disguise could be in worse hands.

I scribble my answers as Freddy asks Yoshi, Aimee, and Clyde for their sizes. When Clyde hesitates to answer, he gets measured, too. Meanwhile, Nora shoos Aimee out to go lie down on the sofa in the break room. "You've had a long night, hon. A nap will do you good."

Quincie pushes off the table to offer Aimee a quick hug first.

"We need to wrap this up," Freddy says as his phone buzzes. "Sergio will be in at any moment." Frowning at his screen, he leaves the room after Aimee to take the call.

Meanwhile, Nora hands an egg-beef-bean burrito to Clyde. "Protein," she says. "It'll calm your nerves. I can fetch some fresh crickets if you prefer."

Quincie moves to give Clyde's shoulder a sisterly squeeze and reassure him that Kieren will be fine. From what I can tell, Quincie's the Wolf's girl. Clyde's his buddy. But they've got their own friendship and history. I'm thinking that's nice until I catch a whiff of blood — pig blood?—and realize Quincie's drinking it from the sports bottle.

What under God's green earth? Has the girl never heard of trichinosis? The Cat in me isn't totally repulsed, but it's disturbingly icky behavior, especially coming from a human. It suggests she takes the restaurant's Goth theme too much to heart.

"Kayla asked about werepeople power," Yoshi reminds everyone.

Nora tilts her head, like she's weighing him. "You can tell her about the coalition."

"I'm no expert on the subject," he admits, reaching for his third burrito.

"You'll do for now," is her reply. I don't know Nora well, but I'd swear she's up to something.

Freddy strolls back in. "That was Karl Richards, the Armadillo king, looking for you, Clyde. He has a lead on the Snake. He wants to talk to you here tonight."

There's an *Armadillo* king? The only armadillos I've ever seen were roadkill.

AIMEE

"DUDE!" Joshua exclaims, drawing Clyde into a back-slapping hug in Quincie's family room. He's been expecting us. He's got a sewing machine set up and stacks of folded clothes on the dining table beneath the art deco chandelier. The next hug is for me, and Yoshi gets a warm handshake. "You must be Kayla!" Joshua gives her cheek a quick air kiss.

"I must be," she whispers, gaping up at him.

Kayla's not the type to gape at a good-looking guy or even a smoldering-hot guy, though she's always sneaking peeks at Yoshi. But Joshua is transcendent, a celestial wonder. From the top of his dreadlocks to the tip of his silver-painted toenails, he's divine.

Literally. Clyde and I figure that he's Quincie's new guardian angel. She's a wholly souled vampire, the heroic and cuddly kind, and her undead state is top secret (beyond us, only Kieren, Nora, and Freddy are in the know). Earthbound angels are supposed to operate on the q.t., too. But Clyde and I aren't stupid, and we're friends with Quincie's previous GA, the angel Zachary (who inspired the marble statue in Sanguini's herb garden). Besides, Joshua's too spectacular to be believable as a mortal, and his belt buckle reads HEAVENLY.

Yoshi doesn't know any of that. It's not my place to tell him or Kayla. Not that Yoshi seems the least interested. He's slipped into antiques-dealer mode, inspecting the colorful rustic rug hanging on the wall behind the television. The handmade baskets and figurines as well as a few of the paintings and rugs were collected by Quincie's late father on archaeology trips to Central and South America. Her parents died in a car accident back when she was in middle school. Nora and (sometimes) Freddy live here now, along with Joshua, who bunks in the attic.

"What's all this?" Clyde asks, picking up a box of laundry detergent marketed to hunters.

"I've been busy." Joshua holds up a black short-sleeve T-shirt. "Charcoal lined. Your odor molecules are supposed to bond with the charcoal."

Smart. With werepeople, scent is everything.

Ever-sensible Kayla picks up a box of dryer sheets and turns it over to study the directions.

"We've got sealable plastic bags," Joshua adds. "Odor-free soaps and shampoos . . . baking soda to brush your teeth with. You'll want to change clothes and shower as often as you can. Freddy is bringing by your other clothes tonight."

Being in a crowded place (like Sanguini's) should make it easier to blend, even more so because of the competing aromas of food, wine, and guests' perfumes.

Before we left the restaurant, Quincie handed me a thousand dollars cash. She said to take off work for the time being in case somebody shows up there looking for me and Clyde.

The upshot? If I'm going with my fave Lossum later to meet Pop-Pop Richards (also known as the Armadillo king), we'll need to look different enough from ourselves that even fellow staffers don't recognize us.

Suddenly, the shifters tense. "Stairs," Clyde says, grabbing a stack of clothes. "Attic. Roof, if we have to."

When threatened, Cats run and climb. Kayla and Yoshi likewise load up, leaving only the sewing machine behind. In a smooth motion, Joshua unplugs it.

From what Clyde has told me, earthbound angels smell virtually indistinguishable from humans. There's a hint of vanilla, but they sweat like the rest of us. So, the remaining problem is me. I've been in the car with two Cats and a

Lossum for *hours* and chowed down first breakfast with a Tasmanian weredevil. A Bear's nose could detect that. "I'll shower."

I'm on the third stair when I hear the knock. Joshua takes his time answering. I've reached the master bathroom when the pounding begins.

Running water mostly drowns out Joshua's enthusiastic greeting as I shimmy out of my clothes and under the spray. I picked Nora's bathroom on purpose. The chef has a passion for heavily aromatic bath products. Apple-scented shampoo, black orchid body wash. Perfect.

I hurry to lather and rinse. I slip on her heavy robe and tie the terry-cloth belt tight. I have to lift it to keep from tripping as I scamper back downstairs, where — as feared — Joshua is offering an angelic, dimpled smile to two 350-plus-pound men I assume are werebears and an officious-looking twit in an FHPU uniform. Joshua's managed to hold them at the front step.

"We received a tip that the owner of this home, one Quincie P. Morris, under the legal guardianship of Meara and Dr. Roberto Morales, employs a Clyde Gilbert at her restaurant up the street," reports a thin male voice. "Do you know him? Has he been here recently?"

Playing dumb, Joshua asks, "What has the boy done wrong?"

No answer. Addressing his burly companions, Agent Masters asks, "What do you smell?"

"Cats, fresh, one's off somehow . . ." is the answer. "Wolf, and lots of it. But less recent."

"I'd love to let you inside, Agent Masters," Joshua says, covering his phone with one hand. "But you can't be too careful these days. You don't have a warrant, and I've never heard of the Federal Humanity Protection Unit. Funny thing, my state senator's office hasn't either."

Huh? *Go*, Joshua. Come to think of it, we've heard no mention of the FHPU in the media. It could be some shadow agency within the government—very Men in Black.

As I come up behind him, Joshua's tone is upbeat. "I'm trying the *Capital City News* now."

I ask, "Are these men harassing you?"

Joshua holds up a finger. "Yes," he says into the phone. "News desk, please."

"Who're you?" The fed peers at my fresh-scrubbed face. "Shouldn't you be in school?"

Joshua is talking to someone at the newspaper who's trying to pull up the FHPU on the Web. "That's right," he answers. "Private property, and they don't have a warrant."

The agent draws his handgun. "End the call."

Joshua does. He raises his hands, stepping in front of me. Are we the first to doubt this so-called FHPU? No. Back in Pine Ridge, Sheriff Bigheart ran into them, and then he and Jess made sure we escaped. Joshua says, "Now, let's be reasonable, gentlemen. You don't —"

The twit fires his weapon, hitting Joshua in the chest. The shot may be quiet—silencer—but my scream sure isn't. I can't help it. It's horrible. It's blasphemous.

Joshua staggers back from the impact, collapsing into my arms. He's a tall, muscular guy, and it's all I can do to break his fall. I glance up, and the gun's pointed at me.

I brace myself, but Clyde, Kayla, and Yoshi drop in full feline forms from the roof, landing hard on Masters and the Bears. A huge risk in a residential neighborhood in the light of day. Pound for pound, a werecat—even a Lion—is no match for a Bear, but my friends have speed and surprise on their side. In the fray, the door slams shut with everybody inside.

I lunge over Joshua, trying to shield him from further damage.

It ends fast. In seconds Agent Masters is unconscious, and the Bears are in chains kept stored in the attic. Yoshi's able to quickly retract his hands to snap the locks in place.

When Clyde raises a clawed paw to strike a Bear, I yell, "Don't! It's not their fault!" At least it may not be, if their behavior can be explained by neural implants. They look lost, baffled. Like somebody pulled the plug. The FHPU didn't give them orders for this scenario.

Yoshi chokes out, "Apply pressure!"

Yes. Right. That's what they do on TV when someone is shot. I press down with my palm, and it's instantly drenched in blood. Meanwhile, my other friends' bodies rearrange. Their bones grind, contract, lengthen, and snap. Their flesh twists like Silly Putty and glistens with a slippery liquid unique to *Homo shifters*. The scent is like a mix of mud and trees and sweat.

Yoshi finishes first and with the least obvious pain. He hurries to bring me fresh kitchen towels to use as a compress. Then he gags the Bears with two more.

I slide Joshua's phone across the floor toward him. "Call Quincie!"

"Quincie?" Yoshi's naked, gleaming. "Shouldn't we call 911?"

Am I sure Joshua is an angel? Yes, yes, I am. What's more, Oliver told us to lose our phones. We've got to be more careful. "No, *get* Quincie." We're at her house, off Congress and Academy, near the state school for the deaf. Sanguini's is only a few blocks south of here.

Joshua whispers, "It'll heal on its own. Take a little time, but . . ." There's so much blood, it's hard to tell if the bullet missed his heart.

Yoshi still isn't convinced, and I don't blame him. "I've got this," I lie. I honestly don't know how an angel's physiology might differ from a human's, but I'm sure we don't want modern medicine trying to figure it out.

"If you say so." The Cat jumps over Joshua, offering an eyeful of his jiggling man parts (I'll *never* be as casual about nudity as the shifters are).

Clyde sits up, a whole lot of naked himself. "This FHPU jerk reeks of yeti."

Kayla, panting, confirms, "He's right."

"Grab his keys," I say. The Bears could tell Joshua's no shifter. They couldn't know he's an angel, which means the FHPU is willing to murder anyone, even a human who gets in their way. If not for my friends, I might be dead.

"Yoshi," I add. "You move Masters's car . . . out of the driveway. Into the neighborhood, not too close to Sanguini's. Then fetch Quincie." I catch myself saying "fetch" to a wereperson and feel lousy about it. A least Yoshi's not a Wolf.

The Cat doesn't seem to notice, though, and is dressed and gone by the time naked Clyde and naked Kayla are steady on their feet. Kayla grabs for the Mexican blanket folded across a nearby tufted chair and wraps herself in it. "Your friend needs emergency medical help, Aimee!"

I wish I could explain. "Easy," I whisper to Joshua, mesmerized by the blood. "You'll be okay." Or at least he said so, and I have faith in him. Angels are supposed to be immortal, but if they're corporeal, they can be hurt. Badly. "You're going to be okay, aren't you?"

CLYDE

CLIMBING THE STAIRS, Aimee scolds, "Don't drop him!"

"I'm *not* going to drop him." I'm carrying Joshua. She's applying pressure to his wound. It would help if hanging baskets didn't stick out from the walls at weird angles. Or if his legs were shorter.

I'm pissed that Joshua got shot, but he's an eternal being. Aimee could've died. My family — my baby sibs — they got an at-home visit, too. Wereopossums are known to be skittish. But not when cornered or when there are young to protect. Things could've gotten ugly fast.

If anything happens to any of them, so help me, I would kill again. There was this human woman, a hunter, on Daemon Island. Rich, like all of them. A sorceress. She shot

Yoshi. He walked away with a scratch, but she was shooting to kill. No, worse than that. She was shooting for trophies. Werewolf heads above the mantle. A werebear-skin rug in front of the fireplace. A Tasmanian weredevil stole.

I didn't mean for it to happen. I started out a broken-down wereopossum. I was caged and useless. The arctic asshats had taken away my crutches. They separated me from all the other captive shifters except Noelle. She was caged alongside me because they planned to breed her.

Noelle's explosive sex appeal, along with the threat of a quickly spreading fire, triggered my first transformation to Lion form. I hauled ass into the jungle to rescue the hunted. What I didn't know was that they'd constructed and camouflaged Burmese tiger pits. I pounced to stop the hunter-sorceress from firing again. She fell into one of the traps. I'll never forget her scream or the way it cut short. She was skewered like a pincushion. One of the sharpened sticks went right through the back of her neck and exited her throat with a chunk of tongue on it.

An accident, sure, but it was still my responsibility. I don't regret what happened. Not exactly. She was a murderer. I acted to defend the others. But, bottom line, I've taken a mortal life. On some cosmic level, I'm in the minus column. The freaking least I can do is not drop a bleeding angel of the Lord God.

"Careful around the corner," Aimee nags as I turn into Nora's room. There's a photo of her son on the dresser. Ferns hang in the windows. Notes from the Sanguini's cookbook are scattered all over her desk. The Moraleses became Quincie's guardians last fall after her uncle died. They were willing to let her stay here, so long as Nora moved in to serve as the responsible adult. It's the only bedroom in the house with an attached bath.

"Should we have moved him?" Aimee asks. "We shouldn't have moved him."

It's too late to worry about that now. Joshua's out of it, muttering about "brushing the warhorses" and playing Pictionary with someone named Idelle.

"Wait!" Aimee whisks away Nora's lacy bedspread, embroidered with bluebonnets. The sheets will be trashed by blood regardless. The mattress, too.

As I lay down the angel, Aimee rushes to the adjacent bathroom for fresh towels. Yoshi hasn't come back yet. Kayla's getting dressed. I already threw my clothes back on.

"Joshua?" It's Quincie's voice, from downstairs. She marches through the door before Aimee or I can reply. Preternaturally fast. Quincie's eyes are red. Her Wolf's down, now her angel, too. "I'll take care of him," she announces with fangs barred. "I'll —"

I slap her face. Hard. "Snap out of it!"

Aimee charges out of the bathroom. *"Clyde!"*

Quincie lifts me by the forearms. A full mane sprouts from my head. My saber teeth descend. "Mif o' 'op o' ebrythin' else, ooo loose or mole, we are oyally kewed."

"What was that?" Quincie turns to Aimee with a raised brow.

"He's trying to say that if on top of everything else, you lose your soul, we are totally screwed," my girlfriend translates. "Or maybe 'royally screwed.' But his throat has shifted too far for him to articulate it."

Quincie sets me aside — like I'm nothing — and rushes to Joshua. She takes her guardian's hand. She brushes his dreadlocks out of his eyes. He's a holy being. A lesser vampire, a soulless one, couldn't touch his blood-stained skin. Not without being destroyed. Quincie is special.

Whatever. I made my point.

AIMEE

DOWNSTAIRS IN THE KITCHEN, Clyde and I try to sell Kayla on the idea that Joshua doesn't need a doctor or, for that matter, the undivided attention of an entire ER. "Joshua is . . . robust," I say. "It wasn't as bad as it looked."

"Uh-huh." It was Kayla who cleaned up the not-insignificant puddle of blood on the hardwood floor. Rinsing the mop, she asks, "How dumb do you two think I —"

"Shh!" Clyde cocks his head. "Someone's coming. It's not Yoshi."

"What now?" the Cat girl whispers.

The sharp knock at the back door is impatient. This time it's a friend. Meara Morales, Kieren's mother. Quincie must've called her. Miz Morales barely nods at us before jogging upstairs with her worn leather doctor's bag. Miz Morales isn't supposed to know what Joshua is either, but at this point, that's between her, Quincie, and God.

"Everything's fine now," I announce to Kayla. "Miz Morales is an amazing healer. She brought Clyde out of a coma last fall." I don't mention that the spell she used blew the roof off of her house. Repairs were finished only a few weeks ago.

"You were in a *coma*?" Kayla exclaims. "What happened?"

"It's been a hell of a year," he replies.

A few minutes later, Miz Morales returns with her bag. "Joshua's passed out from the shock, which is a mercy. I created a patch. It'll hold him until I can figure out something better. For now, I've left Quincie in charge." It's an alpha female werepredator tone (with the barest trace of her Irish homeland), and none of us question her. I'm sure that "temporary patch" is mystical in nature.

I introduce Miz Morales to Kayla. I don't have to explain the Cat-Wolf part. Their noses will tell them that. "Nice to meet you, ma'am," the Cat girl says.

My mom wishes I was that polite. In Pine Ridge, Kayla explained that everyone held her, the mayor's daughter, to a higher standard.

"I have news from Father Ramos," Miz Morales says. She sets her bag by the door and grabs one of the Bears by the shoulders. "Give me a hand, will you?"

As Clyde lifts the same Bear's feet, Miz Morales says, "The FHPU is a fake federal agency. They don't exist."

"You're sure?" Kayla asks, tossing Masters over one shoulder.

"Unless the White House is lying to the Vatican," Miz Morales replies.

Feeling like a weakling, I open the door and look around outside to make sure nobody's around. Then the shifters load the FHPU team into a white van labeled ENDLESS LOVE BRIDAL PLANNING. When Miz Morales isn't healing werepeople, she tames bridezillas and, when necessary, their mothers.

"Of course the FHPU is fake," Clyde says, like he realized it from the start. "Why would the feds care about Daemon Island? It's not a U.S. territory. This is payback from the arctic asshats."

Kayla asks, "What're you going to do with them?"

"The Bears?" Miz Morales checks their pockets. "Turn them over to the interfaith coalition. If they're sellouts, they'll be questioned. If they've been controlled using implants, surgeons will be called in for the extractions and then they'll be questioned."

Something occurs to me. "Be careful. The FHPU . . . or

whoever's behind this . . . could be tracking those Bears right now, using the same chips."

"Noted. Thanks, love." Having found nothing so far, the Wolf healer moves to rummage through Masters's wallet. Seconds later, she holds up a plastic security card with his photo on it.

Clyde looks at me. "It's an MCC Enterprises employee badge." This day just keeps getting better.

Yoshi runs up the driveway, carrying a briefcase. Curious Cat, he's broken the locks. "Look what I found in their trunk!" He opens the lid, revealing two rows of fluid-filled glass vials, half of them with green caps and half with red caps, along with metal syringes packed in foam padding.

Miz Morales pries out a green-capped vial, the side of which reads MCC INJECTIONS and, in smaller lettering beneath that, A DIVISION OF MCC ENTERPRISES. She unscrews the top and sniffs it. "Hmm . . ." Then she tries the red. "They're indistinguishable from transformeaze, but . . . I'm not sure what we've got here."

Transformeaze is a black-market drug that can temporarily halt a shift in progress. It's nasty stuff. The formula is brewed using a demonic spell and can cost users their self-control. The Daemon Island snowmen, working through their dealer Paxton, were local suppliers.

Now MCC is manufacturing something like it? Or was

MCC manufacturing it all along? The evidence is piling up. I might as well be the one to say it. "MCC and the FHPU could both be controlled by the snowmen."

"Pretty elaborate ruse, posing as federal officials," Kayla observes aloud, leaning against the side of the van. "Why go to so much trouble?"

"The arctic asshats routinely hire humans and crooked shifters as front men," Clyde says. "They've even been known to raise demons." He rubs his bristly chin. "Shifters have a long, not-always-friendly history with law enforcement. The arrival of a federal agent would scare most of us into cooperating. Add werebear muscle to that and . . ." He's thinking about his family. "We should take off before they send someone else."

I doubt Quincie will relocate Joshua, but I feel sorry for anyone who tries to mess with her right now. She doesn't only have superpowers — she's got connections. There's a limit to how much hands-on help we get from heaven — something about free will. Still, when she shouts out to an angel, she can count on an answer back.

Miz Morales holds the vial up to the daylight, frowns, and returns it to the case. "Hang on, I'm lost. What snowmen? Aimee, what're —?"

"She means the goddamn greedy yetis." Yoshi opens the door and hides the briefcase under the front seat. "They live to make money off our furry hides."

"The arctic asshats on the news," Clyde says, in an effort to be more helpful.

"Those albino Bigfoot creatures?" Miz Morales asks, retrieving her medical bag. "I thought that was a hoax."

"White fur, but they're not albinos." Clyde slides the van side door shut. "As for the hoax . . . that's what they want everyone to think."

"Let's say these so-called yetis are in charge," Kayla puts in, raising a finger to count off the players. "*Homo sapiens* are their target market. MCC is their corporate arm. The fake FHPU is their strike force. The chipped or sellout weresnake is their front man, and . . . that's all I've got." It's a lot more than we'd put together an hour ago.

Except . . . I ask, "You really think they're working with the weresnake?"

"If their MO is using shifters against shifters . . ." Kayla looks to the boys, who nod for confirmation. "The fact that a theatrical werereptile just kidnapped a state leader to declare war . . ."

"A war that would generate a fortune in sales for MCC's brand-spanking-new product line . . ." Clyde continues.

"Seems like a huge coincidence," Yoshi concludes. "Too huge."

"Excellent." Miz Morales stows her medical bag on the front passenger floorboard.

Really? It's basically my worst nightmare. Clyde and I exchange a look.

Yoshi asks, "Excellent how?"

Hugging me good-bye, the Wolf woman's smile is vicious. "Knowledge is power."

KAYLA

OUR NEW HIDEOUT is a two-and-a-half-story Craftsman bungaloid mansion with a beige stucco facade and dark green wrought-iron balcony rails. Statues of sleeping dragons guard the entrance to the front portico. The inside has been recently restored, mostly appointed with what Yoshi describes as "Stickley furnishings." The fridge is fully stocked. His grams's truck is parked in the detached garage. What my mom wouldn't do to land a real-estate listing like this.

It's another property that Quincie owns. "Inherited" was how Clyde put it. She inherited the restaurant, her home, and this house, too. That's a lot of money in play, but a lot of loss, too. For some reason Clyde won't talk about,

Quincie herself isn't fond of this place and almost sold it a couple of times, but for one reason or another, the deals fell through. Now, with the interfaith coalition's safe houses compromised, it's become useful.

I feel more secure than I have since leaving Pine Ridge. We napped in turns this afternoon. Freddy dropped off burner phones we can use in case of emergencies and warned us that the GPS had been disabled. I'm aching to call Jess and my folks, but I can wait.

The fact that the FHPU is bogus doesn't mean it's not still after us.

From the day I realized my species, I've worried about ruining my folks' lives because of it. Not only their careers — local politics and real estate are all about word of mouth — but also whether they feel safe and welcome in church and at the VA hall and on Main Street.

At almost 8 P.M., I've stationed myself on a landing. It's the intersection of the front stairs, leading up from the foyer and the back stairs, originally designed to connect the kitchen to what I suspect once was the second-floor maid's quarters. Aimee is downstairs in the front parlor, Yoshi in the upstairs library, and Clyde in the attic.

"Come up with me," Yoshi says, appearing above in the hallway. "Or go downstairs with Aimee and watch out back. You can't see much from there anyway."

Actually, I've got a clear view of the nearest intersection.

Joshua's blood is fresh in my mind. So is the memory

of having been shot at last night myself. On the other hand, we don't seem to be in immediate danger, and Yoshi wants a few minutes alone with me. He's not pressuring. He suggested another option, keeping watch with Aimee, and offered the library rather than a bedroom or the sleeping porch.

We've yet to acknowledge between us his declaration of like this morning at his grams's antique mall. Is it too soon after Ben's death to think about another boy that way? It's late April now, and Ben died the day after Valentine's Day.

I can't help wondering what it's like to feel the silky touch of a fellow Cat, and Yoshi's saunter beckons. Not that it's completely physical. I like that he has the same instincts, knows how to work on a car, and helped exorcise my ex-boyfriend's ghost.

I like that, despite his possibly psychotic grandmother, he's got an open heart.

I liked him back when I was still the sweetheart of Pine Ridge. I could smell his desire as we traveled naked, side by side, last night in the car. I can smell it on him now. I've only known him a few days, but I'd known Ben my whole life and look where that got me.

In one fluid motion, Yoshi sets his palms on the broad oak banister and swings down the five steps separating us. It's nothing I couldn't do, but I wouldn't. I'm too used to passing, to hiding everything about me that's Cat. I feel a thrill as his hands rest on my hips. He has none of the doubts a human boy would. He can smell the desire on me, too.

"Hey, kitten," Yoshi says, lightly massaging the small of my back. It's an obvious nickname, but I love it. Is he going to kiss me? Should I kiss him?

I should kiss him. I'm about to when the doorbell chimes, and we spring apart.

Aimee calls, "Stand down." I hear metal rings slide across the drapery rod above the beveled-glass front door, then the unlocking of the deadbolt. Aimee adds, "It's Freddy and Jess."

Jess! "Did she bring my car?" Yoshi calls. She did.

Yoshi uses a burner phone to tell his grams that she can find her truck parallel parked near Blanco and Ninth Street near the Moonlight Tower. He beeps off when she starts cussing him for having taken it in the first place. Then he and Aimee duck out to move his own car — a classic Mercury Cougar — into the garage.

Meanwhile, in the foyer, Jess and Freddy are loaded down with shopping bags. She's also holding a case of supplies from her mom's beauty parlor, and he's carrying a few plastic-covered items on hangers. Raising her arms, Jess asks, "Where do you want all this stuff?"

"Upstairs," Freddy says, taking charge. "The bedroom at the end of the hall."

I give Jess a hand, noticing the Bikes & Babes shop logo. "How're things at home?"

"Peso is at my house," she says, tromping after me up the front stairs. "My family's looking after him, and he's having a bang-up time playing with —"

"What happened to my parents? Are they okay?"

"They're fine, but . . ." Jess's shoulders slump on the landing. "Peso couldn't even go outside to do his business without cameras flashing. Some nut was selling rhinestone leather collars just like his outside your house, and there's a forty-person cult in town that claims you're the ancient Egyptian goddess Bastet."

I admit, "That's flattering, the Bastet part."

Coming down from the attic, Clyde says, "You are kind of goddess-y." Realizing that bordered on flirtatious, he asks, "Uh, where's Aimee?"

"With Yoshi," Freddy says. "They'll be right back."

I've definitely given the neighbors something to talk about. "The media, how's —?"

"Your dad's handling it like a pro," Jess assures me. "Father Ramos stayed to act as a family spokesperson. Everything that's happened lit a fire in your dad. You should hear him. He feels guilty, Kayla, that's he's been so quiet about shifter rights up until now. There's a lot of whispering about what'll happen in Texas politics if Governor Lawson isn't rescued. Oh, and you'll never believe this, but —"

"There's no such thing as the FHPU," I say. "Miz Morales told us."

"They never went public," Freddy points out. "They

97

couldn't. It was a ploy to bully one small-town sheriff and a handful of shifters who'd likely be wary of human authorities."

"They picked the wrong sheriff," Jess says with satisfaction. She adds that the phony feds did, however, manage to get away from Pine Ridge with Tanya and Darby. There's been no sign of Evan, Peter, or Junior the yeti.

"Anyway, they're now wanted for kidnapping and murder and impersonating federal agents." Jess drops her bags on the bed. "Believe me: nothing pisses off real law enforcement like fake law enforcement."

"Daemon Island Inc. kidnapped and killed even more," Clyde points out, joining us in the bedroom. "And did the big, wide oh-so-human world give a damn?"

"The big, wide oh-so-human world didn't know," Freddy (human himself) points out, hanging a few more purchases on a hook on the back of the closet door.

Jess certainly didn't know. She has no clue what we're talking about. "Kayla?"

Werepeople aren't as secretive as yetis. From what I've gathered, our living among, even with, *Homo sapiens* isn't that unusual. But the secrets we keep aren't only for our own protection. Before I was outed as a werecat, my mom and dad led happy, successful, uncomplicated (or at least less complicated) lives.

Is Jess already in so deep that we owe her as much information as possible? Or will filling her in make her a target, too? In the end, I say, "It's not my story to tell."

Clyde goes silent at the window overlooking the portico balcony. For whatever reason, Jess takes that as no for an answer better than I would.

Then Freddy breathes life back into the room by unveiling some of the most spectacular outfits I've seen in my entire life.

MCC Injections has announced the development of a transformation-suppressing patch and vaccine to be administered to shape-shifters.

"We're working with state and local government officials in Texas to make these options available to those shape-changing creatures who have no desire to pose as a threat to the human populace," said Graham Barnard of MCC Enterprises, the parent company.

The patch and vaccine will first be made available on a voluntary basis at pharmacies, medical clinics, hospitals, and private medical and veterinary doctor's offices.

YOSHI

I LOWER THE WOOD BLINDS in the sunroom and turn to drink in the sight of Kayla.

Yowza. It's a hair past 11 P.M., and we're leaving soon with Aimee and the Wild Card for his big whoop de-do secret meeting with the Armadillo king at Sanguini's. Since we're trying to stay low profile, the restaurant is a perfect rendezvous place. An ideal opportunity for disguise.

Exhibit the lady in front of me. Enhanced lashes, cat's-eye eyeliner, and a fake silver spiderweb tattoo that spans her face and another that disappears beneath her gold satin bustier. (I love the word *bustier*.) The skirt is a black ballet tutu, revealing long, long, long legs and high, high,

high heels. I could do without the hair dye, though it does what it's supposed to.

The whole look is designed to draw attention from her exquisite face, to keep anyone from recognizing her as the Cat girl of Pine Ridge.

"What do you think of the color?" Kayla reaches to touch her hair. "People are going to notice a black girl with blond hair, but Freddy swears it's a great distraction. He says no one will recognize me."

I'd recognize her — by sight and scent — but I'm not most people. She looks sexy in a more obvious way. My fingertips play hopscotch between the threads of her tattoo. "I love it."

I've kissed and been kissed by hundreds of girls, mostly human girls. Kayla is molten lava. She slides her hand in the back pocket of my jeans. I'm still betting virgin, but I pray she's not committed to it as a lifestyle choice. We're alone on the first floor. There's a daybed behind us under the arched windows.

Freddy can always fix her makeup. Navigating past the rattan coffee table is tricky. The corner hits right at the back of my knee, jostling my balance, and I break the kiss. "Kayla . . ."

Her hand comes up, flat against my stomach, holding me there. "What am I doing?"

Is this a trick question? "What's wrong?"

"It's not you," she says, and that strikes me as a terrible

way to begin. "This isn't the time." Kayla sinks into a mor-ris chair with embroidered star-pattern cushions and starts unbuckling her shoes. "Freddy got me a pair of lace-up boots, too. I'll run upstairs and —"

"Whoa." I settle on the daybed, rest my hands on my knees. "What are you thinking?"

She's checking me out. "You look striking. Grown-up."

Striking? I'll say. Freddy brought me a black leather-trim Western-style shirt, black jeans, and designer snake-skin cowboy boots. (Take that, Seth!) I haven't put on the steampunk eye goggles yet, but my handcrafted steel cross belt buckle is both Goth fashion statement and precaution-ary. Kayla's gaze lingers there, and it makes me flush.

"Sorry." She shields her eyes. "It's partly Ben. I don't want it to be, but it is."

She misses him. That's only natural. "Listen, kitten, I can wait for —"

"What about Aimee?" Kayla asks. "I know she's with Clyde, and I understand that you and she are close friends. I'm not worried about that. But before you two met, she had a boyfriend — Travis — who died. Now, you're into me, and I had a boyfriend who died, too."

"So, you're saying . . ." I'm tempted to inform her that, from what I understand, Travis and Aimee never hit offi-cial couple status, but that's beside the point. "*What* are you saying? I have some perverse thing for girls who've dated dead guys? Because that's a coinci —"

"No, I'm saying *people die*. Lula died. Your friend Teghan died. Your friends Kieren and Joshua are lucky to be alive. Yoshi, you've been shot at twice in two days. You could die, too."

Hearing Teghan's name stings. The old me, the hit-it-and-quit-it Tom Cat, would've quipped that desperate times are all the more reason to live, hot and sticky, while we can. God, I miss him.

CLYDE

"IT'S BEEN A WHILE." Noelle waltzes into Sanguini's private dining room at five till midnight. The ravishing werelioness was imprisoned in the cage next to mine on Daemon Island. She was my one fling before Aimee. A sultry older woman.

I thought we had something special. Who knows? Maybe we did. Then it turned out she slaughtered my buddy Travis at the local neighborhood park while she was amped up on transformeaze. Noelle was out of it. She didn't even realize what she'd done until Yoshi's sister pulled her off Travis's mauled body.

"What're you doing with Pop-Pop Richards?" I want to know. His Majesty hasn't arrived yet. But Travis was

Pop-Pop's grandson. A "favored prince" of the werearmadillo throne.

A human court might've cared that Noelle didn't know what she was doing. She didn't *intend* to kill anybody. Supposedly, that makes it legally not murder. It doesn't make him any less dead. Shifters tend to skew more primal. If Travis's ghost hadn't interceded with his grandfather on her behalf, Noelle would be toast.

"I'm not here with Richards." Noelle takes a seat at the opposite end of the table. "I'm representing the interested third party." Is it wrong how much I love that costume? She's dressed — blue body paint, dyed red hair — as Mystique of X-Men fame. A shape-shifter disguised as a shape-shifter. She pours herself a glass of ice water. She tosses aside the napkin folded in the shape of a bat and opens an electronic tablet encased in gold leather.

It's only the two of us in here. I set my mask on the table.

Aimee isn't going to be thrilled when she finds out Noelle's tied up in whatever's happening. It's not only our fling. Romance crosses species lines all the time. But there's an extra hormonal, horny *pow* between two shifters of the same kind.

Besides, I was raised as a Possum. I'm new to owning my werelion heritage. Noelle is the only Lion I know. She was with me when I first came into my mane.

"Where have you been?" I ask. "Nora and Freddy were trying to warn you about —"

"I already knew." Noelle stops typing and looks up. "I hid in plain sight at the zoo."

"In Lion form?" Of course in Lion form. It pisses me off when haters call us animals. Noelle and I know what it's like to be caged. But the way things are . . . "Brilliant!"

We laugh together for the first time since our breakup.

I relax my shoulders. Noelle killed Travis, not by choice. I killed Mrs. Great White Hunter on the island, not by choice. Sure, I pounced. Noelle took transformeaze. Neither of us had any way of knowing what would happen. It would be stupid of me to alienate an ally.

"You hear about MCC Injections' new"— she raises her fingers to make air quotes —"'transformation-suppressing patch and vaccine'? It's a modification of the formula for transformeaze. Rather than freezing a shift midway, it blocks one altogether."

Even money that's the poison Yoshi found in Agent Masters's car. Given Noelle's history, I have to give her credit for going there. She releases her claws. "Have you seen their pet troll, Graham Barnard, on the TV news?" She takes a swipe at thin air. "You think he's trying to protect the so-called purity of *Homo sapiens,* or do you think he's in it for the money?"

Noelle has no idea that she's talking about my

107

girlfriend's father. "Well, the human servants on Daemon Island were tricked into . . ."

The Lioness weighs me from behind a curtain of lush eyelashes. "Get real."

Aimee's dad isn't exactly a poor dude from a developing country, desperate to help his struggling family make ends meet. He's a grown-up, big-time all-American corporate flack. "I know him," I say. "Graham Barnard." Or at least we're connected by only one degree of separation. "He's not exactly up with werepeople power."

The slightest limp still betrays Noelle's island injury. With shifters, only the most devastating damage lasts. She rests her palms on the table. "You know Graham Barnard?" Her cleavage is distracting. "You know him how?"

"Doesn't matter," I say. "He's the mouth of the haters. Not the brain trust."

Noelle glances over my shoulder. I turn in my chair, expecting Armadillo royalty. I find Aimee standing in the doorway instead. Her forehead's wrinkled. She clasps her hands in front of her, then lets them fall to the sides. She overheard me and Noelle talking trash about her dad.

"Pop-Pop Richards just arrived," Aimee announces. "Nora asked if you want food." It's a BS question. Of course we want food. We always want food. It's an excuse to check up on me. "I'll tell her yes." With that, she practically sprints out of the room.

Crap. I start to chase after Aimee when Pop-Pop struts in. He's carrying a glass of his preferred single-malt Scotch. (The bar keeps it on reserve.) Two of his rotund royal guards take point outside the room.

"Clyde, what did you do?" Pop-Pop stops me with a couple of stiff fingers to my chest. "Never mind, this is more important." The Armadillo king slides off the jacket of his pin-striped suit. He drapes it over a chair and acknowledges Noelle with a curt nod.

She responds with a hard swallow. The guilt gnaws at her.

I stay put. We need info on the Snake. I'll smooth things over with Aimee later.

A light knock on the door signals Freddy's assistant, Willa. She's carrying a tray of appetizers — gorgonzola and a selection of olives, the carnivore taster, and the wasabi deviled quail eggs. We settle around the table. I pour His Majesty a glass of water as she drops off the plates. Nobody bothers with small talk. Willa lifts her tray and shuts the door as she exits.

Wasting no time, Pop-Pop leans his barrel body forward. "A critical dignitary knows something about this Snake. Important information."

So, it isn't Pop-Pop himself who has the scoop. "Dignitary?"

"He won't talk to me, Clyde." Pop-Pop tosses an olive

into his mouth. "He considers me beneath him, the arrogant ass! But he's heard about your experience with the newly discovered mono-forms."

No more experience than Noelle. She apparently works for whoever it is and is probably his source. "He doesn't want to talk to Yoshi or Aimee?" We were all on the island together.

Pop-Pop lights up a cigar. "I have a confession, Clyde." He puffs. "Did you ever wonder why I encouraged your close friendship with my grandson Travis?"

Noelle studies her retracted nails. She painted them blue to match her Mystique persona. Having shifted to claws and back, they've returned to their natural color.

I spear a piece of venison blood sausage. "Travis and I were like brothers."

"It was fitting that you should be," Pop-Pop informs me. "Two young princes."

"Princes?" I exclaim, dropping the meat. "Uh, my dad is —"

"A fine man," His Majesty replies, waving his cigar. "A Possum for the ages. But I'm not talking about him. I'm talking about your biological father, the Lion king."

Under her breath, Noelle says, *"Hakuna matata."*

AIMEE

POP-POP RICHARDS left half an hour ago. It's almost 2 A.M., closing time at Sanguini's, and Mercedes whisks away what used to be my bowl of kumquat sherbet with frozen eyes of newt. It's on the house, courtesy of Nora.

Security has been quadrupled, with bouncers stationed both indoors and out. Other than a four-top of weredonkeys (whose laughs live up to their reputation) and an aging British pop star (known for his manscara and probiotics commercials), it's been a quiet night.

A man with Mohawk-style hair, sprayed hot pink, winks at Kayla as he sashays by in assless leather pants, and her expression is priceless.

I'm grateful for the distraction. Not that it's completely taking my mind off whatever's going on in the private dining room between Clyde and Noelle.

Noelle. Why did it have to be her? I'm not jealous. It's more complicated than that. I don't blame her for what happened to Travis, not entirely. I don't care that she and Clyde are both Lions and I'm not, at least not much.

It's what they said about my dad. The worst part? I agree with them. He is "the mouth of the haters." But it's one thing for me to say that to Clyde, another for him to say it to Noelle. She doesn't even know my father, and, for that matter, Clyde doesn't either.

All Dad knows about werepeople is what he sees on the news, and werepredators are only mentioned in violent crime stories. I'm sure it's never dawned on him that there are werewolf wedding planners or werecat teenagers admitted to Cal Tech.

The snowpeople may control the FHPU and MCC. But it's not like Dad has any idea that his anonymous corporate overlords are also behind fake federal kill squads. He may be prejudiced, but he's not pure evil.

"Howdy, kids." It's Detective Zaleski from the Austin Police Department. He's a werebear, and he and his partner Wertheimer, a Porcupine-Bunny, are the unofficial go-to men for Austin-area shifters when it comes to all things law enforcement. Zaleski says, "I hear you're in a mess of trouble. Again." Zaleski's not one for cosplay, but he blends in to the extent possible, what with his height and girth, in a tailored charcoal suit. He nods to Kayla. "Young lady."

Zaleski's dating Nora, and I can tell by how he doesn't pay too much attention to Kayla that the chef's already briefed him on her.

Yoshi reaches to shake his hand. "We heard you quit the force." Everyone else at the table can hear the Cat fine, but I have to lean in to catch it. "Over some rumor about —"

"You heard right." Zaleski takes a seat. "I did quit, and I wasn't the only one. Several other shifters called in sick — 'the fur flu,' we were calling it. But the rumor was the rumor."

"Huh?" Yoshi replies. At the same time, Kayla says, "Come again?" She's on her second serving of brandied peaches flambé over French vanilla ice cream.

Off duty, Zaleski sips red wine. "The order really did come down from the governor's office. We were supposed to execute a massive shifter roundup. It was only hours before she was taken, but then there were the obvious facility and manpower issues, especially with so many officers — human and shifter — walking out in protest."

Nice of him to mention those human officers. Too bad Clyde wasn't around to hear it. Unfortunately, I'm not shocked by the governor's order. Shortly before being kidnapped, Lawson also announced that next fall Texas would be doing mandatory genetic testing of public employees and students. On our way here, there was a report on the radio claiming that "Lawson's recent no-nonsense tactics are what spurred Seth and his werebeast followers into action."

Zaleski continues, "Anyway, the governor's kidnapping has taken priority. Bringing her home safe is critical to all of us, especially with that weresnake claiming to act on behalf of shifters everywhere. We've got something to prove."

Sinatra's "Blue Moon" pours from the speakers, and Yoshi asks, "Why would Lawson have ordered a door-to-door shifter sweep? I'd understand something like that as a *reaction* to the unexplained Bear DNA found in the governor's mansion or the weresnake's declaration of war, but it's like she saw all this coming and —"

Zaleski sets down his glass. "How do you know about that? The Bear DNA?"

Oliver. One of the last things the Tasmanian weredevil trooper said to us was "we never met." Yoshi fiddles with his napkin. "You've got your sources. We've got ours."

I'm surprised the detective lets that go, but he's mentoring Yoshi's big sister, Ruby, who's been working toward joining APD herself, and he's got a soft spot for the Cat siblings.

Zaleski informs us that the DNA matched the Bears that Miz Morales brought to the coalition surgeons from Quincie's house. They'd been darted, drugged, and kidnapped out of Washington State and woke up in Texas with the mind-control implants in place. Masters turned out to be a soldier of fortune recently attached to — what else?— MCC's holdings in Afghanistan.

"Good job, kids, taking that SOB down and those chipped Bears, too." Zaleski stands, checking his watch. "You all right? You're quiet tonight."

It takes a moment to realize he's talking to me. "I'm fine."

The detective takes my word for it. "Be careful, and holler if you need anything."

"You do the same," Yoshi replies, and Zaleski grins his approval. Then he's off, striding purposefully toward the crimson velvet curtains that lead to the kitchen and Chef Nora.

The Cats don't comment on my quietness, but Yoshi stretches his arm around the back of my chair. Meanwhile, on the dance floor, the couple costumed as Sally and Jack Skellington twirls one last time. An eight-top of *Walking Dead*–inspired zombies exits through the curtains to the foyer, belting out Sinatra's "I've Got You Under My Skin," and Clyde and Noelle finally emerge from the private dining room. She looks boobalicious in that geek glam costume. Just my luck: Clyde's always had a thing for Mystique.

As she leaves, Clyde maneuvers through the dissipating glittery crowd to our table. He reaches for my hand and leads me to the dance floor.

Whatever happened in there, he's not ready to tell the Cats.

Courtesy of Freddy, the Lossum is dressed in a full Venetian-style joker masquerade mask that adds spark to his pirate-inspired ensemble. I'm in a gender-bending veiled fedora over a double-breasted white men's suit with silver skull buttons and ostrich feather trim — not that anybody would glance twice at two guys slow dancing together at Sanguini's.

"What happened in there?" I ask as Frankie begins crooning "It Had to Be You" over the speakers. With the full mask, I can't gauge Clyde's expression. "Was it about my dad?"

He pauses. "No, not *your* dad."

What happened? We're not dancing anymore. We're standing still. Why are we standing still? "Are you going to tell me?" I ask, half joking. "Or is this a shifters-only secret?"

Clyde breaks the embrace. "A lot of secrets are shifters only . . . or certain shifters only." He walks away. "Being a human, you wouldn't understand."

CLYDE

WE PROMISED FREDDY to only use our burner phones in case of an emergency.

Does finding out my bio dad is the freaking Lion king qualify? It's not like I'm being shot at or a werebear is trying to pull my arms out of the sockets (or is that only a Wookiee thing?). But tomorrow night I'm going to meet him, mano a mano.

My sire, my sperm donor, His Majesty. According to Noelle and Pop-Pop, he's got the lowdown on the weresnake. The king could've passed on the intel through her. He wants to meet me in person. For all I know, he's wanted to meet me my whole life.

At the hideout house, Yoshi is still crashed on the sleeping porch and Kayla is in the bedroom with the front balcony. Too wired to sleep, I offered to stand watch downstairs. My parents should be awake by now.

"It's me," I say when Mom answers. We spend a few moments assuring each other that I'm fine. She and Dad are fine. The kits and my leopard gecko are fine. So are Aunt Jenny and Uncle Victor and the weather in Amarillo. It's in the upper sixties and sunny.

"I don't think it's safe for y'all to come home," I say. "Not yet." There's been no sign of the FHPU since yesterday at Quincie's. We figure they've disbanded. But that doesn't mean the snowmen and their flunkies couldn't come up with a new way to target me through my family.

I called to talk to Mom about the Lion king. I've heard stories about the werelion royalty since I was a kit. Some say they battle to the death for their crowns, others that they're descended from the Lions who sailed with Noah during the Great Flood.

Seated on a bar stool, I start with my other pressing question. "In your text, you said to 'stay away from AB.' You meant Aimee, right? Aimee Barnard?"

"The government man who came looking for you," Mom begins. "He said if you knew what was good for you, you would leave her alone. Clyde, are you dating Aimee?"

I should've mentioned it before. "She really cares about me."

118

"Then I'm sure she'll understand. . . . Possums and humans, it's just not natural."

"What about Possums and Lions?" I reply. "Is *that* natural?"

"You know better than to use that tone with your mother," she says.

"I was a mistake." I've known that for a while. It's the first time I've said it out loud.

"You are a blessing. You're at a transitional age. I don't want to lose you. You're still one of us, Clyde. You're still my son and still half wereopossum."

Now I'm going to sound like a jerk, bringing up my meeting with the Lion king. But I deserve some answers. I hate the idea of walking in clueless. I know it was a lifetime ago. My lifetime ago. My parents were separated, and Dad was off working on an oil rig. Somehow my mom hooked up with a Lion. *The* Lion. "I'm meeting my biological father tonight," I say. "He set it up. He's reaching out to me."

When she doesn't take the bait, I add, "The way I figure it, you two had more than a one-night stand. At the very least, you told him about me. Otherwise, he wouldn't know I exist."

Still nothing. I forge on, leaving out the part about Seth, Pop-Pop Richards, and my friendship with Travis. "What's he like? Why didn't you tell me?"

"I was lonely. He was rebelling against the Pride. We didn't have a future, but I felt I owed it to him to let him know about you. At that point, I went from a dalliance to a source of shame. I never wanted you to see me that way. I never wanted to lose you to your inner Lion."

A toilet flushes upstairs. It's the one off the master bedroom, which means Yoshi's awake. He'll be down here in no time, looking for breakfast. "Mom, you're not going to lose me. I'm happy to be half Possum. Awesome Possum, that's me. It's just that —"

"How many times have you shifted to wereopossum animal form since finding out that you're also a werelion?" Mom presses. "Once, twice?"

"Uh . . ." The truth? None at all.

AIMEE

"RUMOR HAS IT that you're a wereweasel," Winnie Gerhard informs me in the Waterloo High cafeteria. Rather than the lukewarm King Ranch casserole I'm being subjected to, her tray is adorned with a takeout sushi box.

I don't know her well. She's a senior, and I'm a sophomore. Her reputation is more Gossip Girl than Mean Girl, but that's always a fine line.

I glance up from Orwell (my make-up quiz is scheduled for after school) and bare my teeth. "The Weasels are a proud people with close ties to the Armadillos, Rats, and Opossums."

She didn't see that coming. Winnie shifts her weight in her pointy spiked heels.

"What do you want?" I ask. If she thinks implying I'm a Weasel is going to scar me for life, she's out of luck. My boyfriend is half Possum, and he's adorable — usually.

"You and that weresnake Seth aren't going to win this war," she says, pursing her lips. "There's a reason that human beings dominate the planet."

Before I can reply, the newly merged science and engineering clubs surround us and their glamazon president, Quandra Perez, says, "Stop making humanity look bad."

I could handle Winnie on my own, but I'm touched that the S&E crowd is modeling HUG A SHIFTER T-shirts, each featuring a different well-known species (werebear, werewolf, werecat, weredeer, etc.) in animal form. Unlike a certain Lossum, I appreciate the people who're on my side. I let them come to my rescue.

KAYLA

AUSTIN ZOO & ANIMAL SANCTUARY closed three hours ago. It's only us, the animals, and the handful of werecoyote employees who work here around the clock. The young Lion woman, Noelle, picked this meeting place and, as a precaution, sent us on a winding route to get here.

At the gift shop and office, Yoshi handed me a map while Quincie and Clyde reminisced about how their friend Travis's family requested that donations be made to this place in his memory. Then she wrote a big-enough check to fund the whole operation through next summer.

Moments later, as we pass the zoo train station, Clyde whispers, "Do I look —?"

"Like a prince," Quincie assures him.

Carrying the yellow map, I point the way. Along the sandy gravel path, the giant tortoises are unimpressed by our scents and the sleepy tiger merely licks his paw, but the coatis dive for cover and the fancy roosters collide in panic.

There's no question when we see him waiting outside the tall chain-link lion enclosure that we're looking at the werelion king. He's broad shouldered, square jawed, and imposing with streaks of gray in his thick gold hair. He's wearing an oversize gold-and-diamond watch.

Noelle introduces His Majesty as Leander Gloucester. My first time squaring off against royalty.

"I can smell the weremarsupial in you," he says, circling Clyde. "It's a foul taint."

Suddenly, I'm a whole lot less impressed. Quincie's blood-wine cowboy boot inches forward. I can sense the disappointment coming from Clyde. It's not going to be a fuzzy reunion, the king and his long-lost son.

We're here — Quincie, me, and Yoshi — as backup. It's a balancing act, Yoshi warned us in the car. We want to show strength, not suggest Clyde can't hold his own. Aimee wasn't invited. I'm not sure if that was for her protection or because of whatever's going on between her and Clyde. She didn't come back with us to the hideout house last night.

"That 'taint' wasn't a turnoff when you smelled it on my mother," Clyde retorts, fingers hooked casually into his belt loops. "You asked for this meeting. What do you want?"

"I will not be spoken to in that manner by my own lowly half-Possum indiscretion."

I can't help wondering what the resident animal lions on the other side of the partitioned enclosure make of our standoff. There's a white CAUTION sign warning visitors in red letters to STAND BACK because FELINES MAY ATTEMPT TO SPRAY VISITORS. Let's hope not.

At the scuff sound behind us, Quincie pivots to face Leander's . . . bodyguard? He's some kind of massive Cat. I'm guessing six foot eight, 375 or so pounds. If it weren't for his scent, I would've guessed Bear, and a big Bear at that. "Liger," Yoshi observes aloud, filling in the blank.

Half werelion, half weretiger? It's disloyal right now to say so, but cool.

I catch a hint of saber in Quincie's unfriendly smile. I wondered what Clyde was thinking, bringing this human — *is* she a human? — girl.

It may be Quincie's a human-shifter hybrid, and that's camouflaging her scent. Whatever the deal, she's not easily intimidated, even by the Liger. Meanwhile, Yoshi's gaze is tracking Noelle, which gives everybody but me a partner.

Leander folds his thick arms across his rustic linen umber-colored robe — worn, I'm betting, as much for ease of disposal in case of an emergency shift as a status marker. "The Armadillo king and Noelle both tell me that you have grown into an impressive young man, resourceful in a crisis and possessing formidable allies." He gestures to her. "She also claims you burned a multimillion-dollar island enterprise of the ice people to the ground."

Ice people, yetis, arctic asshats, *Homo deific*. For a species that's managed to go so untalked about for so long, they're racking up a lot of names. I wonder again what became of Junior. We haven't seen or heard word of him since Pine Ridge.

"None of that is news to us." Clyde backs away. "Let's go, people."

I'm not sure we should give up so fast, but I don't hesitate. Even Yoshi doesn't buck against Clyde's tone. Solidarity matters. We retreat. Me and Yoshi to one side of Clyde, Quincie to the other, we march four abreast, up the hill past the tortoise enclosure, toward the prickly pear cacti.

"Wait!" King Leander has chased us beyond the fenced-in tiger. "Wait, Clyde."

When he's acknowledged by name, Clyde turns and so the rest of us do, too.

"There is no such thing as a weresnake," Leander announces. "Or, for that matter, a werereptile. The cold-blooded abomination that kidnapped the governor and declared war on humanity is a hell-spawn demon. An old one, from the first generation of horrors that rose from Lucifer's flames."

A demon? As in a *demon* demon? Seth is a scaly evil horned thing with a tail. . . . Not that I'm an expert, but I admit that does fit my personal definition of demon. I'm a devout Christian girl, a weekly churchgoer. I don't want a damn thing to do with demons.

"What kind of demon?" Quincie asks like she knows what she's talking about.

"The worst kind for people like us," Leander says. "A shape-changer himself."

KAYLA

IN THE BACKSEAT, Quincie gives Clyde's hand a quick squeeze. "His loss," she whispers, even though the rest of us can hear her fine.

Up front, Yoshi lowers the volume on a Luminous Placenta song. "You done with him?"

"The Lion king?" Clyde buckles his seat belt. "We got what we needed, or a piece of it anyway. The yetis' loud-mouthed pet is demonic. Kayla, what can we do with that?"

His voice is full of bravado, and he says "demonic" like it's business as usual.

"Me?" I ask as we leave the zoo parking lot. "What do you —?"

"You know about politics," Clyde points out. "You grew up in a political family."

"My dad is the mayor of Pine Ridge. We're not the Clintons!"

The boys and I end up at an outdoor gallery, in the shadow of an honest-to-God castle that's easily walkable from the hideout house. (Clyde says it used to be a military academy.) The street art on display looks to me like high-end graffiti: surreal, colorful images on exposed foundation, erosion barriers . . . I'm honestly not sure what all. It's kind of overwhelming.

In Austin this is culture. In Pine Ridge it would be considered a white-hot mess.

We're in hoodies and loose-fit yoga pants. The idea is to go unrecognized in outfits that wouldn't restrict shifts, but we look like soccer moms. It'd be smarter to go straight back to the house, but all of us need space to breathe, especially Clyde.

We dropped off Quincie at the Moraleses'. She bought a stuffed toy wolf at the zoo shop for Kieren's little sister. Quincie and Miz Morales are trading off taking care of Kieren and Joshua.

Either way, I feel bad for Clyde. Being adopted comes with its share of lingering questions. I'm sure Clyde didn't like the few answers he got today.

I clear my throat as the boys, seated on a concrete

barrier, tear into the takeout fried chicken. They'd better not finish it all by the time I'm done talking.

"Since the FHPU first appeared in Pine Ridge, we've been running. Hiding." I stand like I'm giving a campaign speech. "Because that's what werepeople do. We hide from *Homo sapiens*. Sometimes right in front of their noses, but we still deny who and what we are. Now there's a new — or at least new to us — humanoid species out for our pelts, so we're running and hiding from them, too."

I've pricked the boys' egos, but I have their attention. "The FHPU has been able to abduct and kill shifters in part because of the world we live in. The snake demon and the governor's kidnapping have put everyone on edge. We need to change the conversation. We need a spokesperson people can rally around."

"Who?" Clyde asks, taking a sip of sweet tea. "Kith —"

"Died," I say. Palpate Kith was a werecat, a peace advocate who reached out to world leaders. The Gandhi of shifters, he was assassinated six years ago in front of UN headquarters. No wereperson has stepped up to fill the void. "We get out in front of the media with a Lion king, someone who can challenge Seth and give the talking heads something better to talk about."

Yoshi tosses a chicken bone in the bag. "Leander will never go for it."

"It's not about reality." I stand still and let my arms fall naturally to my sides. It's confident body language. "I'm

130

talking perception. The snake demon is invoking the story of Satan in the garden and linking the fall to werepeople. But in the animal world, lions are viewed as royalty, so when it comes to werelions, humans are primed to assume—"

"*Pfft,*" Yoshi says. "Tell that to the wereorcas and polar werebears."

"The massive werecarnivores are already on our side," Clyde points out. "All we need is a male Lion." He sits up straighter. "Someone majestic." He raises his chin. "Someone inspiring." Clyde's grin becomes toothy. "It doesn't have to be Leander."

AIMEE

I ASKED QUINCIE to tell Clyde that I wanted to meet tonight at the neighborhood park. This is our spot, at the chain-link fence that used to serve as a shrine to Travis's memory.

At first, it was like the whole city turned out to leave homemade cards, signs, and mementos. Then the number dwindled to those of us who knew Travis personally, many choosing armadillo images — small stuffed toy animals and my favorite, a brightly painted *alebrije* of a dillo with wings. Now, it seems like any other hunk of chain link. Life goes on, or so people say. That may be, but the death of someone you care about changes you.

The long yellow convertible pulling in to the lot is Quincie's, but the driver getting out is Clyde. He jogs over and, like nothing's wrong, says, "Hey."

"How did the meeting at the zoo go?" I ask, walking toward the swings.

He follows. "Quincie told you about that?"

Like he's surprised. "The question is . . ." I sit, rocking back and forth. "Why didn't you?" It's not as though my beginner tae kwon do status would impress werepredator royalty, but I hate that he's keeping secrets. "You could fill me in now."

Clyde doesn't move toward the swing beside me. He's not in the mood to play.

I try again, swaying. "You could tell me why you're so pissed off."

"I'm not. I'm trying to figure something out." He combs his fingers through his thick hair. "What would reassure people like you — sane humans — that werepeople aren't scary, dangerous monsters? Especially when people like your dad are selling millions of dollars of products on the idea that we are?"

Are we back here again? I ask how things went with his biological father, and suddenly the conversation is all about mine. "Even if Graham Barnard walks away from MCC — and I'm going to talk to him about that — someone else would take his place."

"That excuses him?" Clyde stops my swing, grabbing

a hanging chain in each hand. "I guess you're pro-shifter when it doesn't cost you anything."

Oh, please. "It's complicated. Werepeople don't live in your own separate world. You live in —"

"Yours?" His claws have come out. His saber teeth are down.

"Ours." I fight the urge to scramble backward off the swing. It's Clyde, my Lossum. He's emotional tonight. Something went wrong at the zoo, and that's not all but . . . "Would it *always* be a bad thing, taking away a werepredator's ability to shift?" I don't mention the big herbivores like the Elk or Rhinos, but they can do a lot of damage, too.

Clyde's eyes have gone gold. "Because?"

"Take young adolescents," I reply. "That's an unpredictable time. You've said so yourself. Or look at those scars on Quincie's hand. Kieren's claws did that. I know it was an accident. But if it weren't for his mother's healing abilities . . . Don't you think he'd give anything to take that back?"

"Do I think Kieren would surrender his free will or Wolf nature to a bunch of arctic asshats and corporate bigots? Not so much, no."

"My dad . . ." Is not a corporate bigot? Of course he is. But I believe people can change, and part of me understands why Dad thinks the way he does.

Last fall, when Yoshi's big sister, Ruby, was working

134

as a spy for the interfaith coalition, she staked a soulless vampire named Davidson Morris (Quincie's uncle, no less). Then Ruby lost herself to her inner Cat to the point that she began lapping up his blood.

Quincie, who walked in on the scene, told me about it.

I was shocked. Ruby's tough, every inch a Cat, but also a vegetarian.

I don't like the way Clyde is looking at me, and I'm fed up with dominance posturing. Prince Not-So-Charming isn't alpha to me. I duck out from under his arms.

"Are you afraid of me?" He sounds hurt. "Seriously? Your best girlfriend is a vampire."

Marching toward home, I clarify, "I'm not afraid. I'm annoyed." He should be able to smell the difference. "Don't bring Quincie into this. It's not her fault, what she is. She's never killed anyone." She doesn't play stupid head games either.

"I didn't choose *this* life," my boyfriend counters, trailing after me. "If I killed someone in Lion form, would that be it for us? Would you just move on to the next boy shifter?"

Now I'm baffled. "What are you talking about?"

"You don't think I've noticed that you're werecurious? Or is it that you're trying too hard to prove you're not like your dad? Not that he's such a bad guy."

I've about had it with Clyde's sarcasm. "My father is not Lex Luthor!"

"No, he's Luthor's flunky. He's the guy who writes Luthor's speeches and announces LexCorp's new kryptonite ray gun and tells the reporters at the *Daily Planet* that Lex isn't available for interviews. Your dad's not smart enough to be Luthor."

I've never heard this edge to Clyde's voice before, but shouting at each other in a public park isn't exactly stealthy. "You've lost your Lossum mind."

"Have I?" he replies as we cut under the canopy of a pecan tree. "First, my buddy Travis the Armadillo, then Yoshi the Cat, and now me. You keep trading up the food chain. You didn't want me when I was a bald-tail weremarsupial. You didn't become my girlfriend until I turned out to be a Lion, too."

"Don't you think you're selling yourself and Travis and Yoshi short? Not to mention, me." I poke him in the chest with one finger. "You're wrong. I *did* want you. You were just too thickheaded and busy lusting after Noelle to realize it."

AIMEE

ON OUR WAY TO WATERLOO HIGH, Quincie fills me in on
the meeting with King Leander and the news that Seth is a
hell-spawn demon — unfortunately, not the first I've come
across. In the snowmen's island kitchen, I worked with a
demon named Cameron.

In reply, I offer Quincie an edited version of last night's
blowout with Clyde.

"'Werecurious'?" As we put the top down on her yellow 1970 Cutlass convertible (nicknamed "the Banana"),
Quincie exclaims, "I cannot believe he said that!"

Me neither, but Leander must've been a huge disappointment. I understand now why Clyde was extra
touchy on the subject of fathers. "His family's in Amarillo.

Kieren's out of commission. I'm the person closest to him, so he took it out on me."

"Eh," Quincie replies. "He could've taken it out on Yoshi just as easily. I'm starting to think they both get off on the drama in their bromance." She adjusts her backpack and slings an arm around me. "You don't have to make excuses for Clyde."

It reminds me of Clyde saying I'm excusing Dad. Is it so wrong to want to believe the best of people you love? At least Dad claims to love me back. That's more than I can say for Clyde. It's been two days since I told him in the car and nothing.

Once we're inside the school, Quincie and her econ teacher Mr. Wu exchange a sharp high five as they pass each other in the foyer. Then we veer at the office and stroll by a SAVE HUMANITY banner featuring a drawing of Seth surrounded by a circle with a diagonal line through it. A janitor is ripping it down, and two girls selling prom tickets at a table are bitching about how the threat of interspecies war is a distraction from the social event of the year.

As arranged, Quincie and I stroll into the library and smile polite *hellos* at Mrs. Levy, an English teacher. She approaches the checkout counter with a biography of Cesar Chavez. Meanwhile, we turn toward nonfiction. There it is — at the end of the second row of shelves where Mrs. Levy left them, Kieren's Spanish-language copy of *The*

Blood Drinker's Guide along with a half-dozen other musty tomes, a few in languages I don't recognize. Probably paranoid, but we didn't want to risk leading anyone to her house.

At the Moraleses' request, his Wolf studies collection has been in safekeeping with Mrs. Levy for the past few months. Quincie carries the thickest books. She also picks up copies of *Teen Vogue* and *Seventeen* from a nearby rack. Trying to be discreet, we slide into a nearby table and prop up the magazines.

Mrs. Levy tacked a Post-it note to a relevant page. After fifteen minutes of nobody paying attention to us, I flip that book open. It's not like my inability to sprout fur or fangs makes me any less capable of research.

I study the illustrations. We've got a snake wrapped around the Tree of Knowledge, a snake standing on two legs, artful use of foliage to protect Adam and Eve's newfound modesty . . . Moving past Genesis, I skim entries on revenge snakes, poisonous snakes, and, on the upside, fertility and medical and ecological snakes. Ancient Greek snakes. Ancient Roman snakes. Kipling. Flipping ahead, the demonology section is exhaustive.

Quincie taps a bit of text: "Snake demons are known for their preoccupation with discord, from individual households to international relations." It goes on to mention the Tudors and Franz Ferdinand. Quincie says, "I'll see what Kieren can make of all this."

Right then Dad — Graham Barnard of MCC Enterprises — walks in and scans the library. I take in the navy suit, blue shirt with white collar, brown horn-rimmed glasses, receding hairline. He looks older than I remember. When did he get back in town? This is not good. Or is it?

We need to talk. He wants me to stay away from Yoshi and Clyde. I want him to stop telling the world that werepeople aren't people, and I need to find out what he knows. Most of all, I need to intercept Dad before he comes over here and gets a good look at these books.

"What's wrong?" Quincie asks. "Hey, isn't that your —?"

"Yeah, it is." On Daemon Island, it made all the difference that I was inside the snowmen's headquarters. Not by choice, granted, but I don't have to be kidnapped to infiltrate MCC Enterprises, and it's our most tangible lead to Seth and the snowmen.

I reach to confirm the burner phone in the pocket of my windbreaker. Standing, I slide the books toward Quincie. "Tell Kayla and the guys that I'm going to talk to Daddy Dearest about a few things and find out whatever I can."

The limo is black and stretchy, a corporate rental with a new-car smell. It's suspicious, Dad showing up and pulling me out of school — even if I didn't fight it. I've barely buckled my seat belt when he turns half of his attention to his handheld.

"I've got a business conference outside of Austin this weekend," Dad informs me. "I thought we could do a father-daughter brunch — I can't tell you how tired I am of Chinese food — and catch up on each other's lives. I'm thinking Mexican."

"How about Tia Leticia's Salsa Bar?" I suggest. "But I should call Mom —"

"I've already talked to her." He sets his hand over the box of files on the black leather seat between us. "Your mother has a huge influence on you, and most of that's wonderful. I freely admit that I haven't been around as much as I would've liked, but I'm still your father. You're still my responsibility. If she's not able to rein in your . . . youthful impetuousness, I have no choice but to step in."

Dad pushes a button on the door to raise the glass separating us from the driver. He's still skimming his e-mail. "It's come to my attention that you've been associating with werebeasts."

I've been expecting this. "Werepeople . . ." I trail off as his expression turns condescending. It's a controversial word, "werepeople." I know Dad thinks it's a stupid exercise in political correctness. The term literally means "man-people." Some shifters object, too, saying it implies that their animals forms are something to be ashamed of. My friends tend to use "shifters" and "werepeople" interchangeably. Nobody close to me except Dad says "werebeasts."

"Werepeople are individuals." Recalling my friends'

road-trip conversation about Wonder Woman and Cheetah, I add, "Some are terrific. Some are terrible. Most fall somewhere in between."

"You could say the same thing about pit bulls or sharks," my father counters, pocketing his device. "Not all of them are dangerous. But I wouldn't want one dating my daughter."

Fine, but Dad has no idea who he's really working for or how far they're willing to go. If I try to tell him that his bosses are really furry white Cryptids and his coworkers include a shape-changing discord demon, he's going to think I've lost my mind. I'll need proof to convince him, along with whatever other information I can pass on to my friends.

"About your business conference," I cut in, as hope dims that I can pry his mind open. "Your company is marketing implants that can control werepeople and a drug that can suppress their ability to shift. Can I come with you to learn more about all that?"

Before he can say no, I add, "It's for my semester report in Mr. Wu's econ class." I'm not taking econ, but Dad wouldn't know that.

YOSHI

"You *let* her go with him?" Clyde exclaims.

"Aimee's father's employer may not be a fan of werepeople, but Aimee herself is a human and his own child," Quincie points out in Kieren's upstairs bedroom at the Moraleses' stone-and-stucco McMansion. "The FHPU never went to Aimee's home or Waterloo High or came looking for her at Sanguini's. Has Mr. Barnard shown *any* sign of being a threat to her?"

"No, I guess not." The Wild Card stops pacing. If it were me or Kayla, he'd still be arguing, but Quincie and Kieren have more influence over him.

The Wolf puts in, "I'd be shocked if Graham Barnard has any idea —"

"Yeah, I know," Clyde admits. "I still don't like him." There's more to it than that. I sense his concern, that's sincere. But he's feeling guilty about something, too.

A few minutes ago, Kieren's mom sent us up with mini cans of Dr Pepper, tiny silver straws, and matching napkins. The Wolf is still bandaged up, and Quincie is seated next to him on his waterbed. Downstairs, his dad and sister Meghan (she's four or five) are playing Wii Ping-Pong in the great room.

Meanwhile, I'm checking out the map on the wall (a seventeenth-century museum-quality lithograph under Plexiglas). Kieren is resting his hand on an old leather-bound book that's supposed to tell us how to defeat the demon. He's a Wolf studies scholar, which means he's an expert on history and magic and the demonic.

(According to Grams, werewolves are an overrated, superstitious species preoccupied with their own moon mythology, but she doesn't think much of me either.)

At Kieren's desk, Kayla is using his computer to research Whispering Pines Resort. It's off 71 on the way to Pine Ridge and, according to the business page of the *Bastrop County Examiner,* the site of MCC Enterprises' corporate retreat.

Looking over from the screen, Kayla adds, "MCC bought the resort in late January." This morning, during our shower rotation, the Cat girl scrubbed off her fake tattoos. She's been wearing a pair of shades we found in a kitchen drawer instead. "This is odd. The neighboring state park has been closed. The website cites fire damage, falling trees. I thought all that was cleaned up months ago."

I come up behind her and nudge the Wolf. "You had something to tell us?"

Kieren tries to sit up and winces. "Mrs. Levy found a reference, saying Seth's mission — or at least that associated with his breed of demon — is to create discord . . . strife. It feeds on it. I found another entry. It was heavily footnoted, riddled with disclaimers. Translation may be an issue, but it looks like no weapon of this earth can destroy him."

"Very Whedon-y," Clyde geek-speaks, sipping Dr Pepper.

"Very Eden-y," Kieren counters. "We're talking an age-old evil with a long history of success and a flare for the dramatic. Manipulative, petty, ambitious, boastful —"

"Consider it handled," Quincie replies, giving the Wolf a quick peck on the forehead.

Then, like the matter is settled, they start chatting about some chick named Sabine from Chicago who recently sent them all friend requests on Catchup.

"Hang on," I say. "If 'no weapon of this earth'—?"

"Quincie will kill the monster," Clyde declares, rubbing his hands together like that solves everything. Realizing Kayla and I aren't convinced, he adds, "Trust me. She kicks ass. She's defeated Count Dracula, Lucifer . . . this smarmy vampire chef named Brad."

"Brad," Kayla echoes. She couldn't sound less impressed.

The Wild Card assures her, "It was a big deal at the time."

Quincie blows her curly strawberry bangs off her forehead. "Lucifer was only partially manifest . . ." At the appalled expression on Kayla's face, she adds, "Never mind. I've got a connection. I'm sure he'll help us. He's experienced at this sort of thing."

Uh-huh. I've about had it with these people and their secrets. With Aimee away, Kayla's the only real friend I have in the group. Last fall Kieren spent a night in Grams's barn on his way to joining a Wolf pack up north, which obviously didn't work out. I don't know why.

Anyway, we stayed up late, talking over a twelve-pack of Coors. We'd probably be like bros by now, but he claims I keep staring at his woman. He's imagining things.

I don't mean anything by it. I swear I'm trying to stop.

Moments later, armed with fresh mini Dr Peppers, tiny silver straws, and matching napkins, Kayla and I excuse ourselves to give the others some privacy. At Meghan's insistence, we go to say hi to the Moraleses' three German shepherds. They're all sporting different colored bandannas in the backyard — a mother, Angelina, and her quickly growing pups, Concho and Pecos.

The dogs are all over Kayla and wary of me, which suggests their reaction is less about our Cat scents than my attitude. "What did you make of all that nonsense?" she whispers. "Count Dracula? Lucifer? They're *kidding,* right?"

Thinking it over, I reply, "I hope not."

AIMEE

THE FOUR-STORY Whispering Pines hotel is designed in a huge semicircle, with the lobby, ballrooms, conference rooms, and signature restaurant in the center as well as two lodging wings to each side, all connected by a long curved promenade. Beyond it, between the parking lot and the Colorado River, there's a fenced-off, under-construction amphitheater and a stand-alone, four-story lodging building that have yet to open for business.

At this morning's buffet breakfast, I learned that ground broke on the site shortly after MCC bought the resort. It'll showcase its own performance troupe as well as musical acts traveling between Austin and Houston.

"Sit here and try to learn something," Dad orders in the partitioned hotel ballroom.

So far, he's escorted me to two engineering lectures and a biochemistry lecture. I've done my share of eavesdropping, but so far nobody has mentioned the FHPU or *Homo deific*.

I don't know what I was thinking. I have no idea how to spy. The only thing I've picked up is that MCC is incredibly paranoid about hacking—probably because they've indulged in it themselves. As a result, they're heavily into face time and obsessive about shredding paper.

"I'm on my own for dinner, then?" I ask. Dad hasn't left my side since we arrived, but I've got a copy of the glossy MCC retreat schedule. Tonight's three-hour session follows this evening's cocktail and hors d'oeuvres reception and is labeled "senior executives only." There's a concurrent one labeled "junior executives only," which basically leaves me out altogether.

"Order room service." Dad straightens his bow tie. He's giving a talk on media relations this afternoon. "I have to step away now. Interview with INN." Earlier, we visited the conference room where he and his staff are fielding media. "I'll meet you here in an hour."

"Have fun," I reply, and he's off to work again.

Dad wasn't always like this. He used to come with me and Mom to classic movies at the Paramount Theater and cooking classes (from fruit pies to wild boar) at Central

149

Market. We'd all have these long talks about everything and nothing — like the secret lives of snails or how people are made of stardust — while camping on Lake Georgetown.

MCC has booked the entire resort complex. The amenities and activities are fairly standard: restaurants, shops, two golf courses, three swimming pools, two hot tubs, a gym, tennis courts, spa, horseback riding, and river rafting. The color palette is softly southwestern — turquoise, pink, peach, and lime green. If I were here with my friends, we'd have a blast.

The service is uneven. Two trays dropped at breakfast, and they were out of bacon. The towels in my bath were hung crooked, and I was missing a tiny bottle of shampoo.

Not that any of that exciting intel is going to help save shifter-kind.

As one fungible-looking gal or guy in a neutral suit approaches the podium to introduce another fungible-looking gal or guy in a similar neutral suit, I remind myself it's *good* news that Dad didn't lead me into the lair of the snowpeople (though the hotel air conditioner is cranked high), the clutches of the FHPU, or the fangs of the snake demon.

He's an ignorant corporate drone seduced by an insanely high salary. But the upshot is I've sidelined myself, just when my friends need me most. When Clyde needs me most.

I make a gratuitous effort to focus as the presentation begins and straighten in my chair as I read the title: "The Boreal Retreat & Recreation Initiative."

Boreal was the name of the egomaniacal leader on Daemon Island, and his headquarters was run much like a hotel — full dining and maid service, even a sundries shop of sorts.

I've only been exposed to a couple of dozen snowpeople, most of them security guards in passing — but for an internationally ambitious, technologically sophisticated, economic powerhouse species, they seem seriously committed to pampering.

The MCC speaker mentions the company having bought up a ton of nearby real estate — an effort made easier by property owners wanting to start fresh after the recent wildfires. He goes on to say that this hotel is among the latest of MCC's acquisitions. "Our cost-saving staffing solution is already in place," he adds. "I'm proud to announce that Whispering Pines is now serving as a test location for diminished-rights employees, drastically reducing overhead expenses and . . ."

The audience bursts into applause, and, within seconds, I'm the lone person seated in the midst of a standing ovation. What on earth is a "diminished-rights employee"?

AIMEE

PASSING DAD'S HOTEL ROOM on the way to mine, I say howdy to the maid in a turquoise-and-peach uniform coming out his door. She has auburn hair, wide brown eyes, and a button nose that reminds me of werefoxes. "Turndown service," she replies in a flat voice.

"Uh, this is my dad's room, and I lost something, uh, my phone. I lost my phone, and I remember using it last when I was in here, and so I'm going to look for it. In my dad's room."

"Turndown service," she says again.

I take that as a yes. I go in and shut the door as the maid moves on.

Dad hasn't been with the company that long, but you'd think from his introductions at the podium that he's been besties with the speakers since boyhood. The conference is a lot of rah-rah, but it's also about consolidating MCC Implants and MCC Injections — not to mention a half-dozen other subsidiaries — into MCC Enterprises proper.

According to the execs, since Seth became a household name, demand for the shift-suppression serum and the brain chips has increased a hundredfold and the majority of the orders are international. Governments around the world are eager to contain "the werebeast threat," and MCC is positioning itself as their solution. North America, the U.K., and western Europe are major target markets, but those bureaucracies move slowly. It's anticipated (read: hoped) that "evolving political developments" (read: Seth's declaration of war) will prompt "emergency expenditures" (read: looser moola). There was much grumbling at the podium about the presidents of both the United States and Ireland questioning the company's motives and condemning the hysteria.

Dad may be a lot of things, but he's not super stealthy. The file box is too big for the room's safe, so he left it under his desk. I figure out the combination (my birthday) on my third try. I've wondered if MCC bought the resort as a security measure. They can do background checks on everybody with a key card, not that the maid seemed particularly on top of things.

Perched on an upholstered bench at the foot of the king-size bed, I flip through the files. Nothing on diminished-rights employees, but I see lots of talking-points memos, product information sheets on the implants and shift-suppression drug, and several world maps, including one of the South Pacific. I recognize Daemon Island as the location of the X.

There's also a printout of a photo of Junior. A girl named Shelby Flores had posted it on her Catchup page in an online album of Pine Ridge Founders' Day images. (She should change her privacy settings.) From the caption ("furry fun"), this Shelby probably assumed Junior was a guy in costume.

My friends and I thought it was Junior who called the FHPU on us. From this, it looks like they came after him. A red stamp on the piece of paper reads ACQUIRED. I flip through recent articles on the *Homo deific* remains found in Kazakhstan and off the coast of Daemon Island. They're stamped ACQUIRED, too.

Another document references "damage control" and features a list of names and status updates. Skimming, I see that the deceased island and carousel shifters are listed as "resolved," the rest as "unresolved," and both Tanya and Darby as "contained." There are names I don't recognize, but Granny Z — under "Madame Zelda" — is likewise "unresolved," so I'm assuming the rest are shifters (and perhaps humans) who knew Junior through the carnival.

All the times I've heard MCC, I never wondered what the initials stand for. According to these papers, it's the Meltwater Crisis Corporation. Their icy hunk of earth, their sanctuary, is disappearing because of us. The snowpeople want to wipe out everyone who's encountered their species firsthand and realized what it was. That's part of their vision of damage control.

Well, I've got news for them. The interfaith coalition should have custody of Junior now . . . and oh.

Aimee Barnard. Turns out that I'm "contained," too.

Am I? What's that supposed to mean? I know that the FHPU kidnapped Tanya and Darby from Pine Ridge. If we're all "contained," could they be at Whispering Pines, too? It's a huge property and only twenty minutes from Pine Ridge.

If they're here, I have to find them. I have to at least try.

These are *my dad's* files. He knows . . . I'm still not sure what exactly, but more than I ever imagined. It looks like Clyde was right about him. I feel like I could throw up.

I put the box back under the desk and glance both ways in the hall before returning to my own suite. The maid is still progressing steadily from room to room. She seems oddly oblivious.

Seconds later new birding binoculars are waiting for me on the puffy white comforter at the foot of my hotel bed. I recognize them from one of the shops downstairs. I was there until close today, sorting through the golfer and trophy-wife apparel for something to wear this weekend. Adjusting the thermostat again, I realize I should've bought a sweater. The binoculars are a gift from Dad, I suppose, for breaks between sessions. Or maybe they're a peace offering.

Think, Aimee, think. If I were holding a weredeer and a werebear prisoner, where would I put them?

Grabbing the binoculars, I peer out the floor-to-ceiling window of my suite. A bonfire down and across the river catches my eye. It's near the water, and we've had rain over the past several days. But that's a huge flame, too near the forest parkland, given our long-standing drought. What I wouldn't give for a Cat's vision.

Hmm, Dad left for the ballroom over an hour ago, and he'll stick around after the session to shake hands and schmooze afterward. MCC has an absolutely-no-hooky rule about the retreat program, so the suits should all be busy. I've got time to investigate now.

I take the elevator downstairs and exit to the rear of the property, taking cover in the shadows of the butterfly garden. I turn at the s'mores fire pit and follow the cement path where it veers off to the riverfront. There's no bridge to cross, the water's high, and the moonlight's dim.

A flash of white catches my eye, and I raise the binoculars. There's too much brush. I drape the strap around my neck and start climbing the nearest tree.

I raise the binoculars again, catching my breath at the scene. Three snowpeople—a male, a juvenile, and a pregnant female — stand side by side with their heads bowed. Two more of their species raise a third, laid out on a platform, to rest over the flames.

It's a funeral pyre. Could that be Frore? Frore, whose braids hung in his eyes and whose yak-potato stew I drugged so my friends and I could steal a boat off Daemon Island? It was his body the fishermen found on that lifeboat. His fellow *Homo deific* stole it back.

I recognize the mourners as Boreal, Crystal, and Junior.

It's a solemn occasion, even if I wasn't one of Frore's biggest admirers.

CLYDE

"SETH MIGHT IGNORE OUR VIDEO," Kayla says for the tenth time as she and Yoshi reposition the breakfast table in the hideout house. "Or claim it's a hoax."

"It is a hoax," Yoshi puts in. "We're trying to pass off Clyde as Leander."

Yeah, we are. The tech's set up and ready to go. If the real Lion king won't step up, this Wild Card prince will have to do. "We can't keep hiding forever. It's past time to shake things loose." I'm hanging bedsheets over the sheer curtains to mute the glare. "Should we mention the arctic asshats? If we say Seth's a hell spawn, doesn't that beg the question of who sacrificed a yak or whatever to raise him?"

"Seth is the scary one," Kayla replies as a grandfather clock bongs upstairs. "Besides, not everyone believes the yetis exist, and those who do —"

"Bigfoot freaks aren't going to help our credibility," Yoshi adds. "But going toe-to-toe with a demon, the clergy couldn't hurt. Nora talked to Father Ramos. Our contacts at the interfaith coalition are ready to hit the airwaves and back us up."

It's a PR war. We're trying to stop speculation that werepeople want to rule the planet. And we're trying to clear us in the governor's kidnapping. If we're lucky, we'll rattle Seth and his friends. I can't resist pointing out, "Snake demons don't have toes."

"Thank you, Clyde." Kayla moves to the kitchen counter. She crosses out a line from her script. "Shorter is better." Chewing on her pen, she asks, "What do y'all think of the word *besmirched*?"

International News Network
Transcript: April 26

Werelion king: Citizens of Texas, the United States, and the world, as king of the werelions and official spokesperson for the pan-wereperson community, I am compelled to inform you that Seth is not a *Homo shifter*. He does not speak for us.

In fact, Seth is a demon, a creature of pure wickedness. He's risen from hell on a diabolical mission to deepen the rift between werepeople and humans because, like you, we are children of God, creations of the Divine.

Seth, you have demonstrated your willingness to communicate via the media. Consequently, I am doing the same. You have kidnapped, assaulted, and murdered werepeople. You have besmirched the reputation of all shifter-kind. You have threatened our human friends and allies.

Enough. As king, it is my duty to resolve this matter. I condemn your actions against Governor Lawson. I challenge you to combat. Name the time and the place, and prepare to be vanquished.

AIMEE

A HOTEL IS a twenty-four-hour business. I set the alarm for 5 A.M., sure Dad won't be up that early. I get dressed, grab my windbreaker, and hustle downstairs. I feel vaguely guilty about how much I love the colorful blown-glass chandeliers and the blown-glass sculptures affixed to the walls; more are displayed on the grounds and in the gardens. I'm drawn to the modern and historic sepia photos of Pine Ridge. I recognize Main Street, the Opera House, the beauty parlor, and of course the Old West carousel on the riverfront.

At the reception desk, I say, "I'm looking for my friends. They're about my age. The boy is gangly-looking, the sensitive type. The girl is bold and tall — really tall for a girl — and has this lush, thick hair . . . like shampoo-commercial hair."

The wiry clerk twitches his nose and uses antiseptic gel on the counter to quickly clean his hands. "Did you lose your key card?"

I blink at him. "No, I'm looking for my friends. Have you seen *any* other teenagers —?"

The clerk twitches and cleans again. "The marshmallow roast begins at sundown."

Huh. Maybe he's nervous. The hotel is hosting a conference for its new corporate owners. Word could be out that I'm an executive's kid. "Thanks anyway."

I exit the lobby through automatic glass doors and hail a bellhop in a lime-green uniform with turquoise piping. "Have you seen a lanky, dark-haired guy or a girl built like an Asgardian?"

"Do you have your claim ticket?" he replies.

I wish I had photos of Tanya and Darby. "They're not with MCC."

The stout bellhop bobs his head. "What are the make and model of your car?"

"I'm not leaving the hotel. I'm . . ." It's like trying to talk to a telemarketer. The Whispering Pines staff has been trained too well. They cling to their scripts.

Back in my room, I discover that the TV isn't working. All I can get is the resort channel, which is alternating between a commercial for itself and the MCC conference schedule. I'm fiddling with the remote when a manila file is slid under the door. I flip it open and skim long enough to realize that "diminished-rights employees" are shape-shifters.

Of course! The maid who does the turndown service is a wereperson. So are the guy at the front desk and the bellhop. They've been programmed not to stray from their job descriptions.

MCC is staffing as many low-level positions as possible, throughout its holdings, with werepeople. The idea is to provide them with food, lodging, and medical care "only if the value of the werebeast is in excess of the costs of the treatment." They'll be kept under thumb with brain chips and shift-suppression serum.

What am I doing? I'm an idiot. I fling open the door to chase down whoever slipped the info to me. I briefly hesitate, realizing I've locked myself out, and barely catch a glimpse of someone in a white full-length hotel robe disappearing through the exit down the hall.

As I sprint to catch up, the maids whose housekeeping cart is parked two doors down acknowledge me with plastic smiles. Within seconds I barrel through the door to spot a hooded, robed figure, breathing heavily on the landing below. As loud as I dare, I call, "Stop!"

Junior looks up. Junior, the snowboy who was raised in a traveling carnival by a fortune-telling werecat named Granny Z. Junior, who outed Kayla in the hugest way possible and reported us to the FHPU. Or did he? He's blinking at me with teary blue eyes. "Hello, Aimee."

I descend the stairs slowly, so as not to spook him. "You left the binoculars."

Homo deific own the hotel. Junior's with them. Of course he could get into my room.

He nods eagerly, his voice guttural yet begging for approval. "And I made sure your room was across from the funeral pyre. I couldn't leave you a message. They're listening in on the hotel phone system."

"You could've knocked on my door instead of sliding the file under it," I say.

He rocks in place. "I was worried that you'd think I was like Boreal and Crystal."

Junior is a few years younger than I am. Kayla and I once trusted him. Even Yoshi and Clyde agreed to keep him close, and shifters can scent out deceit.

Once I reach the landing, I set aside my doubts, trust my heart, and give Junior a hug. "I'm glad you're okay," I say. "I've been worried about you."

"Blizzard is with me, too," he replies. Of course he'd never leave his pet cat.

"What happened?" I ask, pulling away. "What are you doing here? Did you send that video of Kayla to the media? Did you call the —?"

"That wasn't me. It was her." He motions me to follow. "Come. I'll show you."

Junior escorts me outside onto the rear grounds of the resort, along the river, past the butterfly garden and s'mores pit and hummingbird garden and sweeping pastures of bluebonnets and Indian paintbrushes that have been babied through the drought. I ask, "Where're we going? Do you know what happened to Tanya and Darby?"

"The men in uniforms took them from Pine Ridge," Junior replies. "I haven't seen them since. Tanya's strong, though, and she has a temper. Maybe they got away." He raises a finger to his lips, urging quiet, and we pass a few groundskeepers. They don't react at all to the sight of the furry teenage Cryptid. At the fenced-in construction site, a sign reads PARDON OUR MESS.

The chain link is backed by green plastic sheeting, protecting the view from prying eyes. Junior and I cut across the lawn to the river and navigate around the rocky bank to reach the other side. There's the amphitheater, which — despite the surrounding signage and barriers — looks finished, as does the stand-alone lodging building beyond it. Both flow architecturally and are in the southwestern color scheme of the rest of the resort. That must be where they're housing their "diminished-rights employees" and themselves.

Following Junior's lead, I crouch behind the corner of overarching cream-colored canvas that's fastened to the ground. Boreal and Crystal are up front, and so is the demon Seth.

"Payment is due," Seth informs them. "In fact, it's over-due." Raised up, he looks taller than Boreal, over seven feet high. There's another two or three feet of tail resting on the stage. "We have masterminded this chance to redeem your defeat on Daemon Island. When humans obtained specimens of your species, we redirected their fear and attention to werebeasts. Now, where is the tribute you promised?" He's big on using the royal *we*.

"Crystal and I offer the boy," Boreal replies in his gruff voice. "We are the only parents he has."

Junior takes my hand in his big, furry one. He's afraid.

"I make no offer whatsoever," Crystal counters, her hand protectively on her swollen belly. Ah, she's the one who outed Kayla to the world. What, among snowpeople, is a feminine voice could easily be mistaken by human ears for Junior's barely adolescent male one.

Crystal adds, "It's a relief that we managed to rescue Junior before our enemy werebeasts could use him to force us to the world stage. We've had too many near misses lately."

That's what they thought we were planning?

Crystal goes on, "How often have we been disappointed or betrayed, relying on for-hire werebeasts or humans to represent our interests? Junior has lived among them. For a *Homo deific*, his expertise is unique and priceless. Having been saddled with this failure of a husband, I deserve the glory of a successful son."

Seth yawns, revealing fangs much larger than they looked on Oliver's phone screen. The demon says, "You owe us *two* children anyway." He snorts. "*Children*. We are far more costly than an entire herd of your species' go-to sacrificial yaks."

Boreal protests, "I didn't expect or ask for —"

"Nevertheless," Seth says, lingering on the *S*'s. "We shall continue with this project so long as it's compatible with our goals. However, absent payment, we are not in your servitude."

Just what the mortal plane needs, a rogue hell-spawn demon with delusions of grandeur.

"Look what you've done!" Boreal clutches his head. "We can't summon a demon and not pay him. That's courting disaster! We've completely lost control of the situation!"

"Wouldn't be the first time," Crystal replies, wagging her finger. "How many times have I told you to check with me before breaking out the cauldron?"

"You told me to do whatever was necessary to vindicate . . ."

Seth exits after them, chuckling.

I wait until they're out of earshot. What time is it? I've got to get back to the retreat before Dad comes looking for me. "In Pine Ridge, they found you along the river walk?"

"Yep." Junior pushes up on his knuckles to stand. "Crystal and Boreal were going to swoop in, pick me up, and leave Texas that night. Then it looked like their baby was coming any minute, but no." He shakes his head. "False alarm. In the meantime, the doctor says she's not supposed to travel. She's not even supposed to be out of bed."

I feel for Junior. Granny Z abandons him for a new life in Florida. He finally encounters members of his own species, and look who he ends up with. Crystal wants to use him to improve her societal status, and Boreal considers him a bargaining chip. It wouldn't ever occur to them that we wanted to take care of the kid and enjoyed having him around. The snowboy may be young and overly trusting, but the same could be said about me. It doesn't mean we're stupid or useless.

"I have an important mission for you." I reach into my windbreaker pocket and hand Junior my burner phone. "Can you make it to the welcome wall at the front of the resort?"

KAYLA

"WHAT ARE WE DOING HERE?" Clyde asks on Sunday morning in a residential neighborhood in the Hill Country southwest of downtown.

Our Lion king video is viral, and the reaction so far from Seth? Crickets.

I wonder if my parents are at church right now. Until the world found out I'm a werecat, I never would've doubted it. But the way our minister condemns shifters, I'm not sure. We talked about going somewhere else, but it's complicated. My mother grew up in that church, and politicians like Dad have to pick their battles.

Freddy must've summoned us to this new-construction ranch-style house for a reason. It's about twenty minutes from downtown, faced with white stone, set back from the road, and secluded from its neighbors. Our scents spooked a deer when we got out of the car.

Yoshi raises his fist to knock, but a priest has already opened the door.

"Welcome," he says. "Come on in." He's soft-spoken, in his late thirties, and has this remarkable kindness to his expression. "Hello, Kayla. I'm Father Ramos."

"My parents?" I ask, pausing in the doorway. "How are they —?"

"Mayor Morgan and your mother send their love." The priest cradles my hand in both of his. "They're holding to their story that the video was simply a badly timed teen prank."

I'm not Catholic, but it's awkward, talking to a man of God about how my parents are lying on my behalf. Not that I sense any judgment on his part — it's more of a weariness rising in me. I'm exhausted by so much not being what it seems.

Before I can ask, Father Ramos adds, "Peso is home now, too."

"Dog person," Yoshi mutters, shaking his head. "You . . . Whoa."

I track his gaze to what must be the reason we're here: Junior, bustling in to greet us with a fistful of napkins and a platter of fish sticks. "Hi, Cats! I brought you tasty treats!"

"What the frak is he doing here?" Clyde demands.

"Aimee sent him," Freddy replies, cleaning his glasses. "Before anyone says something you'll regret, it wasn't Junior who called in the FHPU or disseminated the video of Kayla."

"Aimee sent you?" Clyde steps forward. "Is she okay? How did —?"

"Hang on." Yoshi grabs his arm. "We have some questions —"

"Take it easy," I say, noticing Junior's furry white cat, Blizzard, curled on a rocking chair. "He's just a kid."

Freddy's phone buzzes. Second later he ends the call and reaches for the remote.

Seth's face fills the television screen. "Good day, human scum. I'm here with Governor Lawson to announce that she will be publicly executed at 9:30 P.M. eastern/8:30 P.M. central tomorrow as shape-shifter subjects around the world — and in our live studio audience — cheer.

"The remainder of this missive is directed to the Lion king. Your Majesty, I am baffled by our misunderstanding and your choice to air it in this distasteful public forum. By all means, please do consider yourself invited to join us in celebrating the true savage glory of werepeople!" His smile is terrifying. "By now, you should know where I am."

Coverage transitions back to the news desk. "Eight thirty?" Clyde echoes. "Whatever happened to midnight? Midnight is spooky, pivotal, loaded with symbolic —"

"Midnight is lousy for live coverage," Kayla says. "Seth thinks in terms of TV ratings."

Blizzard yawns, stretches, and then hops onto the rug, before exiting in search of food.

Father Ramos gestures toward the seating area. "You might as well settle in."

The boys choose the matching wagon-wheel recliners, and I take the rocker.

The fish sticks taste crispy delicious, even better with the tartar sauce.

After assuring us that Aimee's unharmed, Junior fills us in on what's going down at Whispering Pines. He hasn't actually seen the governor, but he's overheard that she's on the property. He explains that the MCC execs are being shuttled out now as chipped werepeople are being dispatched to guard the five or so miles of woodland around the resort.

Junior warns, "They'll tear apart anybody who tries to stop the governor's execution."

AIMEE

THE MCC RETREAT ended at noon, and the suits have been exiting Whispering Pines in airport-bound commuter vans ever since. Beats me where Dad vanished to, but I'm grateful for the chance to slip around the fence to the new lodging building beyond the amphitheater. It's the most logical place at the resort to hold the governor and maybe even . . .

A familiar face peeks out at me from behind a tree trunk.

"Tanya!" I rush to give her a hug. "Are you all right? Where's Darby?"

"Aimee," she replies, her voice flat. At shifter speed, she draws a Taser to zap me. "Every day in every way, I will contribute to the profit margin of *Homo deific.*"

I'm aware of the pampered soft grass beneath my body, the flagstone under my sore shoulder. I ache all over like my body was unscrambled wrong in a transporter malfunction.

The scene onstage is colorful chaos . . . mid-shift werebears riding giant unicycles, mid-shift weredeer bouncing shiny red balls on their antlers, mid-shift raccoons tumbling . . .

Royal blue balloons pop off a mid-shift wereporcupine. Mid-shift weregoats butt horns. Mid-shift wereopossums juggle. They're dressed in bright spandex designed to show off their tails, performing courtesy of neural implants and transformeaze.

Boreal adjusts his spectacles. "Arch your back! Play to the camera! Remove that fabric from between your buttocks!" Addressing Seth, he adds, "We'll open with a brief, dizzying array of acts by the shifter vermin and then segue to your execution of the governor."

With so many species of werepeople showing their fur, viewers at home will assume they're all Seth's followers. That they're being used, humiliated, is simply a bonus to him.

"No, no!" the demon exclaims. "This won't do!" He's weaving back and forth across the stage. "We want something *classic*, something old-school that will permeate the human psyche."

"But *you* said . . ." Boreal consults his clipboard. "I have my notes right here." He's flummoxed. "I suppose we could try a contortionist act —"

"Aren't you listening?" Seth asks, lunging toward him. "We're nixing the whole concept. If you want to revive it as a family-friendly resort attraction, like the *tweet-tweet* hummingbird garden, that's your business. But not for our big moment!"

I can't help thinking hummingbirds don't *tweet* when a mid-shift Fox falls from a trapeze. Is that the maid from turndown service? I gasp at the sound of breaking bones.

Seth's head pivots in my direction. "She's awake."

Snowmen grab my upper arms and drag me, struggling, to the stage area.

"This one broke its neck," Boreal reports, leaning over the fallen Fox.

"Dispose of it," Seth orders, offhandedly. "No time to waste and no healer handy." He raises himself up and rears back as if to strike. "Greetings, Aimee Barnard."

I'm not in the mood for chitchat. "Tell me, Seth, what're you doing with that loser?"

As snowmen haul away the werefox, the demon circles me. "When it comes to exploiting werebeasts, Boreal is one of *Homo deific*'s leading visionaries."

If humans and shifters clash, MCC Enterprises is poised to profit. Stirring up prejudice and fear is Seth's easy path to discord. It's a tidy arrangement. But since Crystal nixed Boreal's sacrifice play by refusing to surrender her unborn child and Junior, the snowpeople have lost control of the situation. The demon is calling the shots.

"I grant you," Seth goes on, "that he struggles to grasp the finer subtleties of showmanship. However, sometimes his efforts are truly inspired. Speaking of which . . ."

With a flick of the demon's tail, Boreal draws back red-and-white-striped curtains to reveal a balding, middle-aged man dressed for success but lashed to a large spinning wheel, painted in a bull's-eye. It's Dad.

AIMEE

DAD GOES HEAD OVER FEET, round and round. His eyes are shut tight. Is he crying?

At least now I know he's not one of the bad guys.

"Stop that," I yell. "He'll throw up!"

"Boreal," Seth calls. "Spin it again!"

"I thought you might fasten the governor to the wheel, spin her, and throw until you . . . miss." Boreal rushes to present Seth with a selection of butcher knives on a literal silver platter. "The circus theme could still serve, and it's already paid for."

"You don't have arms!" I shout. "How are you going to throw anything?"

I try to bite the snowman to my left and end up with a mouthful of white fur. "You are *not* going to kill my father!" I exclaim, spitting it out.

"Silence," Seth says, and a thick, heavy palm covers half of my face.

"Greetings, Mr. Barnard." Arms ending in tapered hands extend from Seth's scaly torso. He throws and misses. His blade strikes wood between Dad's neck and left shoulder. "We instructed you to personally resolve, by which we meant *eliminate,* or contain, your child."

Or maybe Dad was pretending to be one of the bad guys, but he betrayed them.

"I did contain her!" my father insists. "She's not a werebeast. She's not disposable like the others. I brought her here to prove she's no threat." Disposable?

"You think not?" Boreal asks. "Junior is gone! His reintroduction to the human-shifter world could prove the existence of my species. It was up to me to contain him! It would be my failure, my responsibility."

The snowman spins Dad again, and Seth selects another knife to throw, this time missing my father's crotch by two inches. When the wheel slows to a teeter, Seth asks, "Last words?"

"Yes!" My father is hanging upside down. "Let me and Aimee live, and I'll return the *Homo deific* boy to you."

"I don't trust the human," Boreal says. "He's losing his hair and has an MBA."

"You can hold on to Aimee as collateral," Dad tells him.

He's not seriously planning to leave me here and go kidnap Junior. When Mom finds out about this, he can kiss his visitation rights good-bye.

"Think about it. She and I also are the only *Homo sapiens* here. I'm a well-known media spokesperson for a major international conglomerate, *your* major international conglomerate. She's a cute blond middle-class girl child. We would be missed. Questions would be asked. Human authorities would be persistent. Human media would make sure of it."

Demons are known to enjoy deal making and to honor the letter — if not the spirit — of their agreements. Still wielding the knife, Seth circles the amphitheater. "Go on."

Dad brings his pitch home: "I'll return the boy to you. Then you return my daughter to me, along with a buyout, a six-figure bonus, and a full benefits package. As a result, these *Homo deific*, under the formidable guidance of . . ."

Seth's bow is almost courtly. "I am Seth, the Original Sower of Discord!"

"Pleased to meet you, Mr. Seth. Bottom line: Y'all can execute the governor, start an interspecies war, make billions on MCC's anti-shifter product line, and nobody will be the wiser." Who *is* this person who looks like my father?

"Very well!" Seth replies. "Return with Junior — just the two of you — here to the theater in time for the show, and our agreement will be sealed." Seth tosses the butcher knife, and it goes wide. "You have until 8:30 P.M. central, or your 'cute blond middle-class girl child' is forfeit."

KAYLA

ON SUNDAY the sun sets in a smear of tangerine and lavender. I'm seated, cross-legged, on the long-leaf pine floor in the attic of the hideout house, staring out the arched window at the treetops. Leaves bud, blue jays battle, squirrels race. "We're playing into Seth's . . . fangs."

"Yeah," Yoshi agrees, coming up the stairs. "On the other hand, we've got no reason to doubt he'll execute the governor. Our Lion king video is a hit, but most people still think Seth is a weresnake. They don't believe in demons — they don't want to. If Lawson dies and the public buys in to Seth's declaration of war, it won't be phony feds out for our skins. It'll be real ones. And they'll be gunning for anybody who can take animal form."

Yoshi sounds so grown-up and responsible. I was sure, of the two of us, I was the more mature one. I tilt my head at a mournful, distant sound.

"Train whistle," Yoshi muses. "The tracks run along Highway One." He lowers himself behind me, straddles my back with his legs, and rests his chin on my shoulder. "You and me, kitten, we could hop a train tonight, ride it out of town, out of state, out of the country."

It's a seductive fantasy, but . . . "I'm all over the Internet, millions of views already."

"You don't look like that girl anymore." His breath is hot against my ear. "Change your name. We could start over. Or forget me. You can have my car, Kayla. Go home to Pine Ridge, skip the big showdown. Take a page from the yetis. Claim the park video was a hoax. It might take some doing, but you can have your old life back."

True, my future isn't written. It wouldn't be easy, but I might still be able find a way to pass for a human being again. I could, for the most part, go back to the Kayla I was before I confessed my heritage to Ben. Or I could put myself on the line, end up dead tomorrow, and I'll have wasted tonight worrying about it. "I want to do something that matters."

"Me, too," Yoshi admits, his body heavy against mine. "But I'd rather do some*one* who matters."

Did he really say that? I growl, twist to pounce, holding

CLYDE

MOUNT BONNELL ISN'T SO TALL that you can't jog up it. If you're in good shape or a Lion-Possum, or, in my case, both. There's a long limestone staircase, complete with metal handrail. It cuts through the sage and cacti from the curving road to the top.

The summit is popular with tourists. At night the white stone and wood patio looks spooky and sacred. Vaggio Bianchi, the original chef at Sanguini's, his funeral was held here. On that big flattish rock off to the downward-sloping side, that's where my parents got engaged.

his hands above his head at the wrists, our bodies parallel. "We were having a serious conversation."

"I offered you my car!" he replies. "I don't get more serious than that."

We bust up laughing, and Yoshi rolls us, so we're lying side by side. I keep my voice light. "You think we'll be all right?"

"Us?" He stays man-shaped but releases his saber teeth and glossy black fur. "We're too pretty to die." He's resting one hand on the curve of my hip and the other under my breast. "Show me."

Show him . . . oh. That's sexy. I don't have Yoshi's control, but Cats are better at shifting than other werepeople. With superficial features, we can linger seconds longer in between. I showed Ben, and he ran from me, but Yoshi would never do that. I unleash, feral and needy, cradle the back of his neck, and urge his lips to mine.

We shove away the crisis, the clock. I show Yoshi my spots, and he traces them with his tongue. This is how Cats were meant to be. I loop my legs around his waist, sinking into fur, flesh, and friendship. He knows what he's doing, and I've always been a gifted student.

I can't say that I love Yoshi, not yet, but I love all of myself when I'm with him.

I requested this midnight meeting. Yeah, the midnight part was mostly me being dramatic. I'm surprised that Leander came alone. It's a relief, though, that I'm not going to have to throw down with his ginormous Liger. The darkness is no problem. Both my animal forms see well in low light. That ability hangs on.

"It's late, my son." His broad back is to me. King Leander surveys the scattered lights below and across Lake Austin.

My son? Who does he think he is, Darth Vader? "I'm here to talk about Seth."

"As am I." Leander glances over his shoulder. "You had no right to call him out on my behalf. You are not the king of the werelions. I am."

"Like I care. Besides, you're not my father. You're not my king. I was raised a Possum. I'm proud of the dad who's there for me."

"He's not here for you now." Leander turns. He raises a hand to say stop. "Now that you have invoked my name, the Pride fully supports my taking a stand against Seth." Golden fur ripples across his face, his body. "It is expected that I thwart his attempt to stir hostilities between *Homo shifters* and *Homo sapiens.*"

His subjects all believe Leander's playing hero. He's pissed at me for putting his royal ass on the line. I step up on a stone border. "How did you get to be king?"

"By birth right," he replies. "As will my eldest full-blooded Lion son after me."

Good luck, bro, whoever you are. "You didn't fight to the death?"

As he yanks back his shift, Leander's scowl is epic. "We are not animals."

Touchy. Shows how much I don't know about my Lion heritage. "I've battled Dracula Prime," I announce without mentioning that the Count left me in a coma. "I killed a Scholomance-trained sorceress." An accident. "I rode a wereorca in triumph as Daemon Island burned in my wake." I didn't start the fire. The Orca saved me from drowning.

I rehearsed this on the way over. I don't only want Leander to step aside.

I want him to look at me and regret what he's missing.

Channeling *Camelot,* I ratchet up my best kingly voice. "Of the two of us, who is more likely to triumph over Seth? I have no interest in revealing my true self as the victor. Should I perish, you will live on to rule as a symbol of courage and shifter solidarity."

"I've had worse offers." The scowl fades. Leander sinks to sit on the rock wall. "Seth relishes conflict and trades in children. His venom is deadly, excruciating, and acts quickly. He can also constrict, crushing his opponent, a combination that is unusual —"

"You said Seth is a shape-changer." I jump down but remain standing. "Can he morph three heads? Become a machine-gun robot? Turn into supermodel Saffron Flynn? Split into an army of snakes — *what*?"

"Such an imagination." Leander's chuckle is weary. "*The Book of Lions, the Book of Old* refers to him as 'the serpent.' The Sower of Discord, the first of his breed. They say he can take the form of man, but no animal except the snake. The snake is his base form."

"That's it? He can turn into some guy?"

Leander isn't amused. "In man form, he's much of the reason being a wereperson is punishable by death in nations like Morocco, Saudi Arabia, and Singapore. That Iowa state senator who wanted to legalize human-shifter marriage? Seth was the one who released his sex tape with the weregenyornis." The Genyornis are werebirds, originally from Australia. *Homo sapiens*' bias is greater against shifters whose animal-form cousins have gone extinct.

Leander glances at his gaudy watch. "It's even allowed him to infiltrate shape-shifter communities. This isn't the first time he's pretended to be a weresnake. He's indulged his hunger for attention, traveling with shifter-owned side-shows and carnivals."

I'm reminded of the "Man-Eating Snake" carnival poster in Granny Z's cabin. The two snake figures on the Pine Ridge carousel. "Sure, but in battle —"

"It was Seth . . . or another demon of his ilk . . . who assassinated civil-rights leader Palpate Kith," the king declares. "Should Seth slay you, masquerading as me, how will I explain myself to other werepeople, to the Pride?"

"Tell them you came back from the dead," I reply. "That'll do wonders for your rep."

Leander's already rocking a major Aslan complex.

THE OFFICE OF
THE ARCHANGEL MICHAEL
The Sword of Heaven
The Bringer of Souls

To: Joshua
From: Michael
Date: Sunday, April 27

Please be informed that your *Appeal to a Refusal of a Petition for Intervention: Order Arch* has been denied.

The situation you describe does not constitute a Class-A-level emergency, directly involving Lucifer himself and, therefore, meriting the involvement of an archangel.

With regard to your argument, I am well aware that the archangel Zachary revealed himself to destroy the minor hell-spawn Duane in the underground parking lot of Whole Foods corporate headquarters in February.

However, Zachary is on personal leave. As such, I am temporarily overseeing matters related to those guardians, like you, who're assigned to neophyte vampires still in possession of their souls.

In Zachary's absence, I deem his action constituted an exercise in managerial discretion rather than a binding procedural precedent and, once again, refuse your request.

AIMEE

LYING ON THE KING-SIZE BED, staring at the dimly lit ceiling, I'm afraid to sleep and afraid not to. It's almost daybreak, and the governor is supposed to die during prime time tonight.

I wonder if Dad will return Junior in time for the show. It's clear now that he's known for some time that my friends and I were on Boreal's hit list. I'm glad that Clyde doesn't trust my father. I only hope my friends will protect the snowboy and hear him out.

My in-room landline has been cut off, but otherwise Whispering Pines makes for a plush prison. Snowmen escorted me back to my suite. They stand guard outside the door and beneath my balcony. None of the chipped shifter employees we passed reacted to the sight of them, and all of the MCC executives have vacated the property.

The knock at the door is a surprise. It's such a polite gesture, a knock.

I didn't undress for bed, and I don't pretend by throwing on a robe. I check the peephole and open the door to Boreal, cleaning his spectacles.

"Uh-hem," he begins. "Crystal requested you."

"Her name is Drifa," Crystal tells me. The snowwoman is breast-feeding in a lounge chair, her furry feet propped up on a lime-green-and-peach striped ottoman.

The fourteen-and-a-half-pound baby, Drifa, has huge blue eyes and is enormous for a newborn. So is the diaper made from a hotel pillowcase. "She looks like you," I say.

I'm leaving Boreal, who already took off, out of it. They're used to living with human servants. I should know. For a while, I was one of them.

On the island, Crystal never would've bothered having a conversation with me. Here, she offered to split her special-order yak breakfast quesadillas from room service. Maybe she's lonely for feminine companionship. She (and now Drifa) are the only females of her species I've ever seen. The guards and medical team are all men.

"Yes," Crystal agrees. "She has a proper coat of fur." She scowls. "But I don't."

Crystal gestures to a cosmetics case on the dresser. "Bring that over here and open it up."

We're on the top floor of the new lodging building. It features the same kind of colorful blown-glass art and framed sepia photos as the hotel. From what she tells me, the lower levels are more utilitarian, with cheap linens and rooms a fifth the square footage of this one. I pause at the sliding-glass door to the only balcony and its view of the river and wooded grounds. The winding, hilly drive from the highway to the resort took the limo a little over five minutes. The state park is on the other side of the water.

"You don't want to do that, pet," Crystal warns me. "Boreal has werepredators patrolling the forest. The flat-headed werepeccaries are especially vicious, and you are a weak, pink-skinned human, so much ugly skin. It's better that you concentrate on grooming me instead."

What's a Peccary? Does she mean a werejavelina? And my pink skin is not ugly. It's just not covered with hair. Furry Crystal, on the other hand, has no use for foundation, eye shadow, lipstick, or blush. Instead, her case is packed with brushes and accessories — sparkly barrettes, rolls of ribbons, fabric and metal and rhinestone headbands, and an array of head wraps.

I skirt around the chair and set to work on her spiral curls. I hope she doesn't expect me to brush out the fur all over her body. I have zero desire to tackle butt tangles.

I imagine the snowpeople living in high-tech underground ice palaces, but I have only the faintest idea of what their society might be like. At the same time, I can see they're desperate to unravel ours. The suite is littered with news, sports, celebrity, and fashion magazines.

"Will you leave the resort, now that you've had the baby?"

"We would, if Junior hadn't run off. A handpicked management team is scheduled to arrive at dawn to program the werebeast workers with a new control word and reopen the resort. We have to vacate by then regardless." Crystal sighs. "Unfortunately, your great minds are closing in on us *Homo deific*." She says "great minds" like the concept is absurd. "However, if Boreal and I return home with Junior, having secured MCC's financial future, our losses at Daemon Island will be irrelevant. It will be dismissed for what it was, a pet project gone awry."

Never mind the millions Daemon Island made or the werepeople who were murdered there. . . . Boil it down and Boreal's approach here is much the same. Only now he's doing it on a bigger scale, through a pseudo-legit operation, and expanding his market.

"Junior referred to you, a human girl, as his friend."

Crystal sounds puzzled by the notion. Does she realize he was raised by a fortune-telling werecat? If so, has she considered what that might mean to him? Granny Z may have left Junior to marry the Old Alligator Man, but she loved the kid. For years she protected him, and now that I think about it, she didn't leave him alone in the world. She left him with me, Clyde, Yoshi, and Kayla.

Crystal adds, too casually, "By any chance, do you know where he ran off to?"

"How do you know the Peccaries didn't get him?" I sound more nonchalant than I feel. I considered the possibility that Junior might be overwhelmed by his mission, that my friends wouldn't trust him. It never occurred to me that he might not have made it off the property alive.

"He is no intruder werebeast," Crystal replies. "No mere human." She strokes the fur on her baby's forehead. "The shifter vermin in the forest have been programmed to do no harm to *Homo deific*."

Which means Junior could leave and return safely, but . . . "What about my dad?"

She ignores the question. Of course if Dad tries to return but doesn't make it to the amphitheater, they'll still have Junior back and me to do with whatever they want. For the foreseeable future, it looks like playing nanny may be my only way to stay alive.

I trade out the paddle brush for a wide-tooth comb

and try again. "Why did Boreal choose Seth to summon in the first place?" I'm not an expert on demons, but there's clearly a variety of them. "Y'all are pretty committed to a low-profile lifestyle, and if you'll excuse me for saying so, he's kind of a show-off."

"What an astute question!" she exclaims. "Pet, you are a bright one!"

I paste a smile on my face and keep brushing.

"Boreal meant well," she explains. "He always does. Every type of hell spawn has its own bailiwick. The ancient stories tell us that Seth's mission is to sow hostilities between the species of man, which seemed compatible with our various enterprises around the globe."

"But *Homo deific* are a species of man," I point out.

"We're only distantly related to humans." She laughs out loud. "You are all such children. We recall a time when *Homo sapiens* and *Homo neanderthalensis* edged on breeding compatibility. Like horses and donkeys. Our species is further apart from yours than that."

Is it? I'm tempted to ask her about the "breeding compatibility" of *Homo neanderthalensis* and *Homo deific,* but it's smarter to keep my mouth shut.

"Boreal had every intention of riding herd over that vile creature on the assumption that I would agree to surrendering our offspring in trade." Sobering, Crystal reaches into the case, plucks out an oh-so-darling sparkly green barrette, and snaps it around a lock on top of Drifa's head. She adds, "*Homo sapiens* cannot be trusted with primary guardianship of this planet. We have no choice but to manipulate your society's commercial and political systems to improve your environmental protocols. Once werebeasts become a servant caste, we'll all be relieved of fairly compensating them. Those profits will buy the influence we need."

Slave caste is more like it. She may have a point about the environment. I could see where global warming would panic snowpeople. But the ends don't excuse the means.

Her matted fur is sticky. *Ew,* is this pink stuff bubble gum?

"We're not inhumane," Crystal concludes. "We'll provide food, shelter, do selective breeding. They'll be given no reason to rebel like on Daemon Island."

No free will to rebel either, what with the brain chips. Was *this* how I sounded to Clyde? I shouldn't antagonize her. I can't help myself. "Would you want to be selectively bred?"

"I was," she replies, steepling her thick fingers. "My mother chose Boreal for me because of his ambition, imagination, and work ethic." The baby starts fussing. "She believed his interest in demonology would prove useful. She agreed with him that deepening the divisions between your people and the werebeasts would prove profitable. *I* would have selected someone with better eyesight and more pronounced genitals."

Gah. I have no idea what to say to that, but she's still talking. "The only reason I've come along on these past two endeavors is that he cannot be trusted to act unsupervised. Once Boreal has made amends to the Assembly of Matrons, I will personally tutor Junior to be presented to highborn peerage females. He lacks sophistication, even by what I understand to be human standards."

Assembly of Matrons? As in ladies? Female *Homo deific* are the dominant gender?

"Poor Frore," I reply, remembering that he was her brother and Boreal's cousin (small gene pool). The funeral pyre must still be fresh on her mind. On the island, Crystal took up for Frore when the males clashed. "He certainly paid for Boreal's ambition."

"Yes." She gently bounces Drifa to soothe her. "Such a loss."

I reach for a round brush. "After he agreed to be implanted with a brain chip, too."

Suddenly, I have Crystal's undivided attention. "What are you talking about?"

I take my time, smoothing curls at the base of her thick neck. "It was in the news," I explain. "When his body was found on that life raft and brought to scientists. They discovered the chip when they examined his remains."

Crystal stands without warning and plops the baby

against my chest. "Take Drifa to the bathroom. She needs to be changed. Be certain to wash all of the excrement from her privates."

I'm going to count that as a win anyway.

THE OFFICE OF
THE ARCHANGEL ZACHARY
The Sword of Souls
The Champion of Redemption

To: Michael
From: Zachary
Date: Monday, April 28

Thanks for babysitting my guardians while I'm on leave during my honeymoon.

My assistants Vesper and Nigel have sent word that, despite our understanding, you blew off forwarding me any nonroutine formal requests from the angel Joshua.

I know my personal appearance in the Whole Foods parking lot was in violation of *The Archangels' Code of Conduct,* and I've apologized to the Big Boss for that.

But guess what? Under those same guidelines, I can still do whatever I want when it comes to my own weapon. So I've lent my holy sword to my former assignment, the vampire Quincie P. Morris. She has previously wielded it successfully and can be counted on to be discreet.

Besides, there's nothing you can do to stop me because you're not my supervisor anymore.

P.S. On behalf of my bride, ascended soul Miranda Shen McAlister, the monogrammed towel set is "lovely and most appreciated."

YOSHI

AT THE HIDEOUT HOUSE, we use Joshua's odor-free soap and shampoo. We brush our teeth with baking soda. It's nothing we haven't been doing every day, a couple of times a day, since returning to Austin. Except this time, Kayla and I pull on charcoal-lined black T-shirts and tear-away warm-up pants, washed in hunter's detergent. We tug on running boots.

We're soldiers now.

It's a hair past sundown at Pine Ridge R&R, a bed-and-breakfast on the outskirts of Kayla's hometown. A half-dozen log cabins are appointed with copper birdbaths and river-rock stepping-stones. Paper lanterns hang from branches. "This was my mother's big listing," Kayla says, undoing her seat belt. "It's been on the market at 1.2 million since last fall."

"I bet the interfaith coalition bought it," Clyde muses aloud in the backseat.

Next to a converted barn with a screened-in porch, five SUVs are parked side by side. They're big; they're expensive. They can each comfortably transport several werebears. Next to Quincie's yellow convertible, another long, low vehicle is covered by an army-green tarp.

I say what we're all thinking. "Aimee should've checked in by now."

"Aimee never should've left with her asshat father in the first place," Clyde grumbles.

I glare at him in the rearview mirror. "If you hadn't —"

"It's none of your damn —"

"Enough!" Kayla scolds. "You can argue about it after we're all dead."

I park my car alongside Quincie's, graze Kayla's wrist with my fingertips, and get out.

Grams bursts from the porch at the same time. She's leading three dozen men and women, most of them shifters, dressed like us and carrying gas masks. Five — make that six — are buck naked and empty-handed. They look alike — protruding noses, weak chins, and bony shoulders.

Werebirds. Before our eyes, feathers sprout from their skin, their arms contort, their legs retract, and beaks erupt from their faces. Their scent becomes fishier, brine and yeast. It'll take a few moments for their feathers to dry.

As Clyde climbs out of the backseat, my nose takes inventory of my allies . . . slightly more men than women (two who're menstruating, nobody who's pregnant), a handful of old folks. Most of those suited up are werebears, including Zaleski, plus Wertheimer, a weretiger couple, three pygmy wereelephants, a couple of Buffalo I recognize from a bar fight (no hard feelings), Leander's Liger, the Armadillo king Karl Richards, along with four of his personal Dillo guards, and a werebeaver, which doesn't sound intimidating until you imagine the world's largest rodent gunning for your ass.

Then there are the humans — Freddy, Roberto Morales, and others I don't recognize. A skinny guy in a turban is bent over a leather-bound book, whispering to a woman wearing a Waterloo High T-shirt. I make out the words *foretold* and *sacrifice*.

Because I've only seen him on television, it takes me a moment to place the man in the rumpled suit, carrying a briefcase. That's Aimee's dad, Graham Barnard.

Clyde recognizes him right away. "Where is she?"

Barnard holds the case over his chest like a shield. "I *had* to leave her. Seth and Boreal would've killed us both if I hadn't —"

Clyde's in mid-spring, his clawed hands extending toward Barnard's throat, when Grams's boot meets his gut. The Wild Card goes down hard, skidding on the gravel drive.

She snarls, "If that's the best you've got, boy, it's a good thing you're the one riding in fancy." Before I can say anything, she gets in my face. "Be grateful I don't kick you for taking my truck without permission."

Freddy offers Clyde a hand up. "Noelle, would you come with us, too?" He leads them toward the building, calling, "Mr. Barnard? This way, please."

"About Aimee," I begin. "What —?"

"So far as we know," Freddy says, "she's alive and will remain so until she can be rescued from the discord demon and the *Homo deific*."

Quincie — ungodly sexy (and Joan of Arc) in a hooded chain-mail jacket over her black clothes — holds the door for them as she exits the porch.

Blocking my way, Grams points at Kayla. "It's past time you high-tailed it home, young lady. I promised your parents we'd have you back by now."

"What?" Kayla exclaims, reaching for my hand. "No, I'm going with Yoshi."

203

Grams will hear none of it. "You're not ready for this, little girl. Take a look around. These people are professional law enforcement, trained private security, and seasoned interfaith coalition operatives, many of them former military."

"What about Yoshi?" Kayla counters.

Grams looks me up and down. "Yoshi survived the jungle hunt on Daemon Island, and nobody cares much whether he lives or dies except his big sister, but she's biased."

"I care," Kayla protests, and I stroke the back of her hand with my thumb.

"Well, then." Grams gets in her face. "You want to get Yoshi killed, protecting you? Because, believe me, he's stupid enough to do that."

I am. I really am. I'm also distracted by the Birds. How does the old saying go? If it walks like a wereduck and talks like a wereduck . . . Not that there's such a thing as a wereduck anyway. They've shifted enough that I can make out their species — six turkey werevultures and ten wereteratorns. The Vultures are local. Their heads are red, and their dark wings appear tipped in white. Teratorns are originally out of Argentina, distantly related to an ancestor of the condor that died out in the late Miocene. Their human-form noses are ginormous, and their bird-form wings span up to thirty feet.

"What about Quincie?" Kayla wants to know. "She's —"

"*I'm* the senior operative here," Grams says. "And I'm telling you no. This is no time for amateurs. Now, be a good kitty and scamper home."

YOSHI

MY GRANDMOTHER MARCHES to open the back of one of the SUVs and motions me over.

"That wasn't condescending," Kayla says. "I don't want to leave y'all like —"

"Don't worry about me," I say, putting my arm around her. "Nine lives, remember?"

"That's house cats," she whispers with a kiss.

"Yoshi!" Grams hollers. "You in or out?"

I'm in. Roberto Morales comes over to offer Kayla a ride home.

I sidestep the full-bodied Dillos, giving Richards a quick salute. Some people may joke about his species, but he's ten times the king Leander is.

"Your gas mask." My grandmother tosses it my way. "You'll have to stay in human form to wear it, and if you don't, the incapacitating agent will mess you up." She hands me a shoulder holster with a tranquilizer gun and a waist-band holster with a Taser gun. "You'll have to stay man-shaped to use these, too." It's a strategy call, prioritizing that evolutionary wonder: the thumb. Grams asks, "You want chain mail?"

What if I have no choice but to take Cat form? Best to shift buck naked, but at least cloth tears easily. "No," I reply. "What do you mean, incapacita—?"

Grams plugs my mask into an oxygen bottle and secures that with buckle straps against the small of my back. "Our werevulture scouts confirmed Junior's report of shifters patrolling the woods and the adjacent state parkland. Over a hundred heat signatures. Based on their speed, they're not humans or yetis. We're sending the Birds back out to drop knockout gas."

She wags her finger at me. "Avoid tooth-and-claw combat. Avoid physical contact — period. Get where you're going, fast, with minimum fuss. Once you hit the resort's main guest area, you should be able to breathe freely. Wind permitting. The Birds are skipping that section so as not to tip 'em off, but watch out for *Homo deific* security."

I buckle the waist holster. "What aren't you telling me?"

"Aren't you a smarty-pants?" If she were in Cat form, Grams's ears would be flat against her head. "A dosage of gas sufficient to knock a Bear or Moose off its hiney would kill a smaller animal-form shifter like a wereraccoon or wererat. We had to dilute it. Anybody weighing in over 175 will feel woozy, but they might still be dangerous."

That's why I have the dart gun: to give anyone still swinging a booster dose.

Grams goes on to explain that we would've gone with a preemptive strike, but coalition chemists didn't sign off on the knockout gas formula until about a half hour ago. "For everybody else, the goal is to reunite the captives with their families, packs, herds, and whatnot. Not you. You back up Quincie. Get her through safe."

Grams startles me with a quick hug. "You're not absolutely worthless," she mutters. "But I still like Ruby better."

CLYDE

"I WAS WRONG," Aimee's dad admits. "There are greater threats to humanity than werepeople." He still considers us a threat but uses the more PC "werepeople."

Barnard sets his suitcase on a cedar log table. He opens it to reveal vials marked MCC INJECTIONS. The case, the vials, they're identical to those Yoshi found in Agent Masters's car. "This isn't the new suppression drug. It's an improvement over the original black-market transformeaze," Barnard informs us. "More stable. MCC biochemists solved the problem we were having with behavioral side effects."

Barnard loads a vial into a syringe. He reaches for my arm.

I ask, "Why should we trust you? Are you going in with us?"

No reply. He'd only get in the way, but . . . "You don't deserve Aimee or her mom either."

He has the grace to look ashamed. "I know."

"Do you trust me?" Freddy asks, taking the syringe. His tone is light, but there's an undercurrent to it. We need to focus. "You can't speak in full-Lion form; you can't pass for Leander in human form. Without help, you can't hold in between for long enough to accomplish anything."

I don't have much choice. "Do it." I grit my teeth as he slides in the needle.

Freddy strides across the wood-plank flooring. He shakes hands with Barnard. "Thank you for your valuable contribution. We'll bring your daughter home safely."

I'll bring her home safely.

Barnard shrinks back a bit, passing Noelle as he exits the building. He leaves his briefcase of poison where it is.

I watch him go. "Freddy, promise me you're sure that whatever —"

"The transformeaze in your system was analyzed in the newly established interfaith coalition lab in Cedar Park." Freddy sets up a standing trifold mirror in the corner. "We've studied its chemical composition, and in theory —"

"Analyzed?" Noelle enters the patio. She brought Leander's car for me to use. "How long has Barnard been —?"

"I get it." I rock back on my heels. "You injected me with the transformeaze that was on Agent Masters." That's why there was time to analyze it. They switched the brief-cases. "What's the point? Why bother to make nice with Barnard?"

It's Noelle who answers. "He's trying to help. There's hope for him, and whether it means much to you or me, it might mean the world to his daughter."

"What's more," Freddy adds, "there's the mother lode of documents incriminating MCC Enterprises in the file box he brought with him."

CLYDE

YOSHI—decked out in black leather holsters and cool secret-agent weapons—strolls into the barn. He takes one look at me and cracks up. "Nice pants."

"Nice grandmother." According to Freddy, they're "amethyst" harem pants. The zebra-trimmed robe, fastened at the neck with a gold medallion, matches.

I'm also sporting the priciest digital watch money can buy—its face surrounded by yellow gold encrusted with yellow diamonds. On loan from Leander, his signature bling. It's been synchronized with the runners' watches distributed to the rest of the team.

"Yoshi has a point," I admit. "I look ridiculous."

With a smirk, the Cat wanders over to study the relief map of the resort property and parkland. His smug expression turns intent. I'm glad he's partnered with Quincie. They'll be there for Aimee, if I can't. I'd been stressed enough about her hanging out with her dad at MCC's retreat. But this . . . he *left* her there with them. It's the difference between taking a routine guided tour of LexCorp and being held captive by the Legion of Doom.

"The pants leave room for a Lion's tail." Freddy hands over a chunky jeweled leather belt. "Purple is the color of royalty, and to add the finishing touch . . ." He attaches a satin purple cloak around my neck. Raising the hood, Freddy says, "So you don't panic any innocent drivers you happen to pass on the road."

Freddy plucks a slim silver flask from inside his tailored suit. He takes a swig of it and begins coughing. "Hundred-ninety-two-proof Polish vodka," he chokes out. "I'm regretting it already." Gesturing to Yoshi, he adds, "How about we give the Lions a moment to compose themselves?"

I wait until the swinging porch door shuts behind them. When Noelle and I broke up, I never imagined this in our future. "Why are you working for Leander? What do you do for him anyway?" I need the conversation, the distraction.

"It's prestigious. It's a paycheck." Noelle stretches her arms over her head. She's not self-conscious about her body the way human girls (and human-raised Kayla) sometimes are. "Technically, I'm his chauffeur. Not the most interesting job, but it's not all bad. I get to drive a reproduction 1935 Supercharged Auburn Boattail Speedster, and Antonio is a beast in the sack."

"Antonio?" I echo.

"The Liger general. He's sympathetic to you, being a Wild Card shifter himself."

He's a *general* now? Werelions don't only have a monarchy. They've got an army. Leander could've supplied more muscle for this operation. But then more of them would know it's not him, off to face the monsters. I restrain myself from making the Tony the Liger joke. "What about your career?"

Noelle's wearing a black Gothic military coat and pants with a cap. "My what?"

"That's why you got hooked on transformeaze in the first place, right? So you'd get more attention in the underground club scene?" I tracked down Fayard & the French Horns on the Web and listened to some audio clips. "Sanguini's could use a singer who knows how to purr. After this is all over, tell Quincie — the redhead in chain mail — that I said so."

We've got to hurry, except . . .

The shift's not coming.

What is this, performance anxiety? Part of me wants to ask Noelle to wait outside, but she has experience with transformeaze. "Something's wrong. I don't feel any to do about my newfound fame. "I wonder how many of my potential future classmates will choose to go elsewhere rather than study with me."

"I wonder how many will choose Caltech because the school has let it be known that shape-shifters are welcome on campus." It's the kind of thing the dad of two hybrid Wolves would say, but he doesn't push it.

Instead, Dr. Morales asks for directions to my house. It's a short drive past the water tower, through fields of corn and cotton, into the old neighborhood. He says, "Here we are!"

Home. It's been a long week away. The media has given up on my appearing. For now, they've moved on. The front door of my white Victorian opens, and Peso darts out. I thank Dr. Morales, get out of the van, and kneel as my Chihuahua flings his hyper, wiggly body at my shins.

I don't have helicopter parents, but I can't blame them for hovering. I don't even mind it — up to a point. I'm still dressed for battle. It's not far from the B&B to the outskirts of the resort. Is Yoshi waiting for the Birds to drop the knockout gas? Is he already in the woods?

"I missed you guys," I assure my parents in the foyer. "But my friends . . . I have to know what happens. I'll be watching in my tree house on my laptop."

"Pumpkin," Dad begins in a firm voice. "You can

different. Amped up, but . . ." My stomach aches where Yoshi's grandmother kicked me.

Noelle extends her claws. She runs the backs of them across my shoulders. It feels better than it should. She asks, "You're used to forcing the shift, suffering through it. You know why your friend Yoshi is so fluid?"

Do we have to talk about him right now? In a robotic voice, I ask, "Why is my friend Yoshi so fluid?"

She whispers in my ear. "He's embraced his feral side. He's confident in his manhood."

Okay. "Look, I'm flattered. But getting it on with you is not going to make me more confident." Though it might do wonders to release tension . . . Never mind, never thought it. "Also, I, um, have a serious girlfriend."

The Lioness laughs. "*That* was presumptuous. I'm talking instinct, community, pride."

"I don't need riddles," I say. "I need . . . step one, step two."

"Step one." She turns my chin with one finger. "Look in that mirror."

I see golden fur, golden eyes, my mane.

KAYLA

THE MORALESES' VAN is overloaded with hand-painted parasols, oversize baskets, glass jars, antique-looking birdcages, silver and mauve pillows . . . "What is all this stuff?"

Dr. Morales pushes down some mauve tulle that overflows onto my seat and starts the engine. "It's for the wedding Meara's coordinating this week at Umlauf Sculpture Garden."

All around us, coalition operatives are converting the B&B into a hospital. Mrs. Morales will be leading a medical team onto the resort grounds. They'll be dropped off three minutes after Yoshi and Quincie. Chatter centers on removing neural implants from the kidnapped shifters, but they're preparing to treat injuries, too.

Meanwhile, Junior arrives with Father Ramos as Noelle and Clyde — what an outfit — exit the screened-in porch. I catch sight of Yoshi in the crowd. He's laughing and twirling around a girl who looks so much like him that she must be Ruby. (She'd *better* be Ruby.)

"That's Yoshi's sister," Dr. Morales confirms. "She and Brenek . . ." The professor gestures to a huge young guy who's suiting up. "They didn't want to risk getting held up at the border, so they snuck into Texas in a hot-air balloon."

Dr. Morales backs the van out and pulls onto the country road. "We have a lot in common, Kayla. I'm a professor of electrical engineering at UT, and from what I hear, you're on full scholarship next year to Cal Tech." He winks at me. "You do know that Texas has a perfectly good engineering school right here?"

I suspect that's not all we have in common. He smells human to me, which means we're both the only one of our respective species in our households. "I wouldn't be surprised if my scholarship offer has been withdrawn," I say. "Now that the world knows . . . or at least is wondering if I'm a werecat."

Dr. Morales shakes his head. "On Friday the California Institute of Technology added the protection of werepeople to its nondiscrimination statement. It's expected that more academic institutions will follow suit."

I caused that. The fact that I'm supposed to be in the next freshmen class meant that they had to figure out what watch TV in the parlor." They're both former military — air force — and an order is an order.

"Don't make me." I appreciate them so much more on account of Aimee's dad and Yoshi's grams. I decide to be honest. "I can't feel everything I'm feeling about what may happen tonight and be the perfect daughter, the first daughter of Pine Ridge, for you, too."

They exchange one of those psychic parent looks.

"Be yourself," Mom tells me. "Be Kayla, whatever that means to you, and we'll always be proud." Shaking her head, she laughs. "Look at that blond hair!"

"I like it," Dad puts in. "Why not try something new?"

AIMEE

"COME ALONG, PET," Crystal says, carrying Drifa in a sling across her body.

It's almost showtime, and so far there's been no sign of Dad or Junior. I've kept my ears open. Most of the *Homo deific* guards and medical staff have already left by helicopter, but no one has arrived. In the meantime, a chipped shifter at the Whispering Pines guard booth is turning away prospective guests, saying the resort is all booked for a private high-security event.

In the amphitheater, the trapezes are still dangling, but the spinning wheel has been rolled behind the curtain up front, along with the juggling pins, throwing knives, oversize tricycles, and other props. The circus is off, at least for tonight.

Instead, the stage has been redesigned to look like a coliseum.

Two electronic message boards have been hung from the open-air metal rafters. A communications console has been positioned on a riser to one side of the audience. Mounted video cameras will capture whatever happens next.

"So much for Seth's Cirque du Shifters," I mutter. No sign of him or the governor yet either.

"It's talking again," Boreal says.

Crystal replies, "It's vocal, but smart for its kind and eager to please."

Every seat is filled by a silent wereperson in mid-shift. Transformeaze plus brain implants at work. From what I've overheard, some are kidnap victims, others purchased through the same illegal trade that supplies the vampire royalty and aristocracy with its "bleeding stock."

It's hard not to stare. I hate to admit it, but I can see the sideshow appeal. Few humans are trusted by werepeople with the secret of their species. Even fewer have witnessed a shifter holding between human and animal form with the aid of the drug.

I'm fascinated by the variety of species — Rats, Otters, Sloths, Buffalo — in the amphitheater. Some of them I can't even identify in mid-shift. What will this look like to humans who don't know any werepeople . . . or at least think they don't? The ones who have no idea their mail carrier is a Rhino or their dentist is a Rabbit. Those who'd never imagine their child's soccer coach likes to howl at the moon.

"I see you pulled in some of the werebeasts from the woods," Crystal says.

"Predators," Boreal explains. "They're scarier to humans."

He moves to center stage to warm up the crowd. "Werebeasts, repeat after me: Every day in every way, we will contribute to the profit margin of *Homo deific*."

The mid-shift audience intones: "Every day in every way, we will contribute to the profit margin of *Homo deific*."

CLYDE

I RECOGNIZE the slumped-over guy at the Whispering
Pines guard booth as Darby. A coalition field team will
bring him back to the B&B. I'm relieved that he's okay. I
never bonded with the Deer, but he's been through enough.

My plan is simple: Seth asked for Leander. He'll get
me and not know the difference. I'll stall and distract him.
Quincie will save the day. Then I'll make up with Aimee.

Leander usually travels with his entourage. But to
avoid outing themselves, they'd need transformeaze injections, too. No way is Noelle going back on the juice, and I
don't trust any of the others.

I shouldn't have said Aimee's father wasn't smart
enough to be Lex Luthor.

He's not. But that's not the point. I should've cut her some slack. Look at how I puffed myself up, trying to impress the Lion king. His attitude toward my Possum parents isn't much better than Barnard's toward werepeople.

The private resort road is narrow and winding. According to Noelle, this car is worth more than half a million dollars. I'm barely going twenty miles per hour. I'm not supposed to look like I'm in a hurry. Kings don't rush.

Metal clangs against concrete. In the rearview mirror, I spot a werejavelina tossing Leander's bumper to the side of the road. She takes off running after me. Javelinas are nothing to mess with. They can clock over thirty miles an hour.

I hit the accelerator. Two steps later, she wobbles and keels over. Knockout gas.

Moments later I cruise by a spa on my left, a restaurant to my right. I pull in to the main hotel entrance. There's no bellhop to open my door or take my keys.

It's like the resort has been abandoned.

That's when I hear it: "Every day in every way, we will contribute to the profit margin of *Homo deific*." It's muted, rising from somewhere between the parking lot and the river.

I stroll along the front walk, beyond the golf carts for shuttling guests to their cars. I turn at a fenced-off pasture of skittish draft horses and donkeys. They're huddled against the far side of their enclosure. My arrival does nothing to calm them down.

The amphitheater is in sight. The wind carries dozens of shifter scents. Bear, Elk, Raccoon, and Rabbit. A hint of the arctic asshats.

The grounds are softly lit by wrought-iron lanterns hanging from wrought-iron posts. The underground sprinkler system kicks on to water the lush green grass and wildflowers.

No one in the crowd reacts to my entrance. I stroll up the center aisle. I'm flanked on both sides by a huge variety of werepeople frozen in mid-shift. They've been given a Transformeaze injection and are being controlled with brain chips. It's like they're toys that somebody forgot to wind up. To my right, I spot Aimee seated behind a media console. She's positioned between Boreal and Crystal (I recognize Crystal by the huge furry boobs and the baby.)

Not to be a diva, but, hey, I dressed up. I'm supposed to be royalty.

Shouldn't somebody be paying attention to me?

"Good evening, Leander." Seth slithers in from stage left. "I see you've reconsidered your stance against transformeaze."

Leander had a stance? "I have a human-form identity to protect." I position myself, feet planted shoulder-width apart, arms crossed over my chest. It's a kingly pose.

"So you do." He tilts his scaly head. "Clyde Gilbert."

At my name, Aimee exclaims and Crystal scolds, "Hush."

Seth announces, "Earlier today King Leander Gloucester of the Werelion Pride sent an emissary offering you, his bastard son. All he asked in return is that I publicly renounce my claim to weresnake identity, release the governor of Texas, and abandon the *Homo deific*."

"When you say 'offer,' what're we talking?" I want to know. "Am I supposed to wax your scales? Polish your horns? Shovel your demon poop?"

"You'll be dragged to hell. Screws will be twisted into your skull. Torture wheels will shatter your bones. Skin beetles will devour your —"

"Will you keep talking? For freaking eternity?" I spread my arms wide. "Because that *would* be torture. But, hey, I'm all yours."

"Clyde, no!" Aimee yells. Crystal hushes her again. One of their armed guards moves forward from the back of the room to threaten her into silence.

"How noble!" Seth takes a sweep around the stage. He's apparently inspecting the decor. Fake white architectural columns have been positioned in a semicircle in front of an ocean-blue cloth backdrop. "How inspiring!" He laughs. "Alas, I refused Leander's offer for the same reason I would have refused Boreal's. Neither cares enough about their children for the offering to rise to a sacrifice."

I glance at Leander's showy watch (8:28 P.M.). I wish I could let Aimee know that the werebirds dropped the knockout gas over the woods ten minutes ago. The coalition teams were dispatched five minutes afterward. Quincie should be here at any second.

"Now I'm giving you a choice." The demon slithers to confront me, nose to nose. In a mocking voice, he explains, "You, in all your Lion king finery . . . Either you agree to slaughter the governor, for the world to see, or I'll kill a certain perky but pesky human."

Frak. Seth swivels his head toward the media counsel. "Bring her."

A guard hauls Aimee away from Crystal. He shoves her between me and the demon. Aimee regains her balance. She blinks up at me and mouths, "I'm sorry."

So am I. Where the hell is Quincie?

YOSHI

"THE KNOCKOUT GAS should have taken effect by now," Quincie whispers, abandoning our hiding place behind the Whispering Pines Resort welcome wall. She's saying it as much to herself as to me. "Clyde should be inside the amphitheater."

Zaleski and Wertheimer just carried an unconscious Darby out to Grams's SUV and reported they're "pretty sure" they weren't caught on the security camera, which has been disabled. Grams is redeploying them a couple of miles east, along with Miz Morales's crew.

Standing, Quincie points to the flock of werebirds as they retreat in the night sky. I've never seen more than a couple fly at a time. It makes me wonder what the world was like when there was room for *Homo sapiens, Homo shifters,* and even *Homo deific* to all live the way we pleased — together or in total isolation.

Quincie and I are one of the last pairs to be dropped off along the perimeter of the resort property. Most got a three- to five-minute head start.

"One question," I say. "Grams said you requested me for your partner. Why?" Ruby was impressed. Grams, too, I could tell. I'm sure Quincie would rather be going in with Kieren, but he's still far from a hundred percent.

"Aimee trusts you," Quincie explains. "So do Nora and Freddy, even Clyde. If this whole thing goes south, I've got secrets I'd rather share with you than with any of the available grown-ups."

The Wild Card cruised out in one of Leander's vintage cars. He'll keep the demon busy until Quincie can do her heroic thing, whatever that's supposed to be.

I don't want her to think I'm hitting on her. I really don't want her to tell Kieren later that I hit on her. But it makes sense to ask, "Do you want me to carry you?" She can't weigh much, and with my Cat strength and speed, we can move faster that way. Freddy offered us an armored SUV, but even yeti ears can pick up an oncoming motor vehicle. Better to slip in unnoticed so we can case out the situation before charging in.

Quincie adjusts her breath mask like it's a nuisance. "Try to keep up."

We take off on foot, not so full-out that we can't be mindful of our surroundings, but fast enough to leave a human Olympian in the dust. We blow past the 19 MPH speed-limit sign.

Yowza. I don't know Quincie that well, but we've got a best friend in common. Aimee never mentioned her doing any serious athletic training. It could be one of Quincie's "secrets," but why?

It's awkward, running with so much gear. This is crazy. We're racing through woods peppered with shifters whose brains are locked on "kill." That thought pushes me faster, and Quincie has no trouble keeping up.

The private driveway from the highway to the resort campus is a nightmare . . . lots of curves and blind spots. Under a streetlight ahead, I spot a female figure lying in the road. "There!"

"I see her." Quincie lowers her voice. "Should we be talking?"

I shake my head. Many species of shifters have great hearing. Our footfalls might be marginally quieter, taking the bordering grass, but the ground is uneven, and we'd risk tripping and injury.

When we reach the unconscious woman, I see she's in her early twenties. From her scent and features, a werejavelina, as they like to be called in the Southwest. Hog women have formidable hips, breasts, and shoulders — plenty of fleshy goodness to lose yourself in. Pre-Kayla me might've asked her out once all this was over. "No dart. The knockout gas must've got her."

"She smells awful." Quincie takes off her mask and drops it to the ground.

That's natural for the species and the reason werejavelina herds tend to live in isolated communities like gated subdivisions. Even humans can pick up their scent.

I carry the Javelina off-road and set her behind a guardrail in the wildflower-dotted grass. It feels wrong to leave her, but our assignment isn't retrieval. "Are you sure about that?" I ask, gesturing to the mask. "I doubt all the gas has . . . dissipated."

"I'm good at holding my breath." Checking her watch, Quincie urges, "Come on."

I love how optimistic everybody is that our strategy will unfold according to schedule.

In the distance, I hear a skirmish off to our right. "Should we check out —?"

"No," Quincie replies. "We investigate *nada*. Stay on target. Everyone's counting on us."

Counting on her, she means. God, she's bossy — fast and bossy. She probably didn't want to partner with any of the grown-ups because she'd have to be respectful to them.

I understand that the girl is impressive. How many teenagers own their own restaurants, inherited or not? She's sexy in a not-trying-to-be-but-radiates-it kind of way, and she's got a badass Wolf boyfriend who's almost as smart as Kayla. But how does any of that translate into demon hunter? Especially when you've got your pick of trained operatives?

We blow past a horse crossing. The next hill is steep enough that even my gorgeous glutes feel it. If I'm remembering the map correctly, the resort complex is in the valley right below.

We're running in sync, me and the coalition's chosen hero, when I decide to go with it. These people know what they're doing. Maybe Quincie's one of Clyde and Aimee's comic-book superheroes. God knows they talk about her like she's Wonder Woman.

Does Wonder Woman have a sidekick?

Does this make me Wonder Girl?

Hang on. Where'd she go?

Holy crap on a cracker! She's in a heap on the road, steps behind me. "Quincie!"

I rush to her side, discover the tranquilizer dart piercing the back of her knee, and yank it free. One of ours . . . friendly fire?

I don't see, hear, or smell anyone, though the wind carries the lingering scent of the Javelina. I pull the chain-mail hood away from Quincie's face and brush back her curly bangs. She fell hard. There's blood in her hair. A shifter could shake it off, but . . .

My fingertips find her throat. No pulse.

KAYLA

"WELCOME, YOUR MAJESTY LEANDER," the snake demon begins, centered in my screen. He's wearing a head-set microphone, like he's a pop star at a concert. "I'm so pleased that you've come to recognize that there can be no lasting peace between humans and shifters. *Homo sapiens* must be punished for their atrocities against our kind."

The feed is live, telecast on every network and all over the Web.

The spotlight swings to a mid-shift Lion dressed like Aladdin — it's Clyde against the Roman-style architectural columns and the turquoise-blue material behind them.

A second spotlight illuminates Governor "Laughin' Linnie" Lawson, her head and hair high, her red dress suit

"Come on," I whisper, trying her slim wrist. Still nothing. She's not breathing either. My partner for less than five minutes, have I already lost her? I risk raising my voice. *"Quincie!"*

It's no use. She's dead and so is our master plan.

and makeup flawless. In one hand, she clutches a Bible over her heart. In the other, she grips a leather whip.

Seth laughs. "Look what we have here! A Christian. A Lion. How old-school is that?" Addressing the crowd, he commands, "Werebeasts, display approval of tonight's execution! Show thirst for blood sport!"

The mid-shift audience leaps to its paws and hooves, howling, bleating, snorting, screaming, barking, and bellowing in apparent ecstasy. No sign of Aimee or the yetis. If they're on scene, they're being kept off camera. Seated cross-legged on a throw rug in my tree house, I can't look away. What on earth is Clyde thinking? His ruse was never supposed to go this far.

What happened to Yoshi and Quincie? Something's gone horribly wrong.

A poster of Montgomery Scott stares benevolently down on me. If the *Enterprise* were threatened, what would Scotty do?

Peso springs off the smiley-face beanbag to bark rapid-fire warning. My Cat ears recognize the way Jess climbs to my tree house, how she grips the midway branch with both hands and swings one leg up, how she says "oomph" once she reaches the base.

At the tree-house entrance, she asks, "Are you watching?"

"It doesn't make sense." Why did I let myself be driven away? I'm no soldier, that's true. I was scared, but no more than I sensed from Yoshi or Clyde. My new friends need me. "I have to go."

"Go . . . what?" Jess replies. "We're going where?"

"Not us," I reply, powering down my computer. "Me." I'm caught short by the flash of rejection on her face. It's worse because I've made her feel that way before. By way of apology, I explain, "It's my fight."

Peso's hopping, his tail whipping back and forth. As I brush past her, Jess grabs hold of my arm. "Kayla —"

"They're at Whispering Pines Resort," I explain, breaking her grasp. Exiting the tree house, I add, mostly to myself, "I'm an *Acinonyx jubatus sapiens*. I can do this. I'm just as much of a shifter as the rest of them. I can run like a cheetah and —"

"Kayla, *wait!*" Jess calls, as I leap to the grass below. She dangles a set of keys. "We'll still get there faster in my dad's car, especially if we turn the flashers and siren on." She glances down at my Chihuahua. "Should we leave the dog up here?"

YOSHI

I DUCK, covering Quincie's body as a tranq gun flies at my face, the stock winging my right shoulder and skidding to a stop across the pavement. "Ow."

When I raise my head again, I'm surrounded by giant werejavelinas in mid-shift form — snouts, glazed beady eyes, a half dozen of them, male and female, closing in from all sides.

"Hi, guys!" I say, pointing. "The Big Bad Werewolf went thataway."

That's the thing about having a mind-control chip shoved into your head. No sense of humor. I throw Quincie's body over my shoulder, and a Javelina charges out of the shrub cover and stumbles up the pavement. He grunts, rubbing his short tusks together.

I might be able to dodge past them to the trees, but not carrying Quincie. She'd tell me to stay on target, to leave her body here. No way am I going to do that.

The Javelinas turn their thick heads, staring into the darkness behind me, unsteady on their feet. Someone's coming. With my luck, it's a stampeding herd of weremoose.

No, it's a black-and-white cop car, Sheriff Bigheart's car.

"Yoshi, *jump!*" That's Kayla voice, coming from the front passenger window.

I spring straight up, not as high as I'd get without Quincie, but high enough to land on the roof of the squad car, and grab hold of the light bar as it crashes into two Javelinas.

"Sorry!" Jess calls. I hear her double-check with Kayla about shifter healing abilities.

"Raise the windows," I yell, remembering the knock-out gas. Superheroic Quincie might've wanted to risk it, but Jess is driving a moving vehicle.

"Oh, right," I hear Kayla mutter.

As the glass goes up, Jess floors it and shouts, "Hang on!"

CLYDE

IT LOOKS LIKE monsterpalooza in the amphitheater. I take a clawed swipe at the governor. Her mascara's smeared. She's sweating through her red suit jacket.

Seth and Boreal asked for drama. They ordered me to put on a show.

I chase Lawson around the arena. My saber teeth snap and salivate.

I can't stall forever. There's a gun to Aimee's head.

With a crack, Lawson's whip slashes my furry golden brown chest. It's true what I told my mom. Since finding out I'm a Wild Card, I haven't taken Possum form. But I haven't had a chance to master my inner Lion either.

I've had to be more careful, if that's possible. An urban Possum, even a big one, could be written off as an animal. An urban Lion wouldn't.

Black leather breaks my nose, and blood gushes out. The governor knows her way around a whip. She's gotten in a few good licks. I knock the Bible from her hand. It flies into one of the architectural columns. I can only imagine how that's playing on America's screens.

The whip cuts across my eyes. It splits my right lid. Fresh blood clouds my vision. My claws catch the governor's arm. I rip her sleeve, catching the skin beneath. Damn it!

"You may kill me, beast!" Lawson clutches her wound. Her voice is magnified by the lapel mic. "But you'll never destroy my faith or the spirit of the people of Texas."

It's just short of a campaign speech. She's putting on a brave face. She believes Seth's declaration of war is real. She believes I want to kill her. The whole world must believe it.

"Enough, Leander!" Seth calls. "End this now."

I can make out Aimee's frantic voice, rising up, begging me to stop. I can't. I'm trapped.

I'm . . . I . . . Color and chaos blur. I can't focus. My inner Lion attacks. Lawson hits the ground. She gasps. The cries of the eager mid-shift crowd sharpen.

Prey, my Lion thinks. No, *enemy.* His jaws close over its lips, nose. Locks its mouth shut. His saber teeth puncture burnt, bitter flesh.

The Possum inside plays dead. The boy inside collapses.

I reject the foul-tasting meat. I throw back my mane. Raise my misshapen forearms and paws in victory. I roar, *only* Lion now.

YOSHI

I LOWER MYSELF from the roof of the squad car and rub my aching shoulder. "You're saying Clyde might've already killed Lawson?" It makes no sense. Leander's car is parked in the circle drive ahead of us. The rear bumper is missing. We are running a couple of minutes late.

That could've made all the difference.

I lay Quincie's body in the backseat, and the glow coming from her holster catches my eye. Baffled, I glance up at the streetlights bordering the circle drive in front of the hotel's main entrance. Then I lean in, seeking the source of the reflection.

Kayla and Jess are still talking, but it's as if from a distance. I hear the word *hurry*. I don't mean to ignore them, but I can't look away from the Light. I rush to the other side of the car to reach it. Slipping off my breath mask, I open the other rear door. What is this?

I slip one hand beneath Quincie's shoulder to raise her slightly, and my other closes around a metal grip. I draw the weapon, a sword, and hold it up. Gleaming gold, the hilt fashioned to look like wings. I'd swear it's handcrafted, priceless. "You think we should —?"

"Yes," Kayla replies as Jess comes around from the trunk with a gray blanket to position over Quincie's body. Kayla adds, "Now, Yoshi."

The sword's magnificence is almost mesmerizing. Kieren said "no weapon of this earth" could kill the demon. If not this earth, where did it come from? "Because?"

Kayla looks like she's about to leave without me. "When you're off to battle hell spawn and you come across a glowing sword, you take it. You'd know these things if you read fantasy or went to church. Jess?"

"Sorry, sweetie. I'm a big fat no on stealing from dead people. Big. Fat. No. On the other hand, I'm not her. This Quincie girl might be disappointed if you didn't finish the job she died trying to do. It's your call, Yoshi. She's your partner on this mission. What do you think?"

Me? I'm a part-time antiques salesclerk, marginal high-school student, and Grams's target practice. Werecat, sure. Devastatingly good-looking. But you could say the last of Kayla, too. On the other hand, I'm betting the sword is one of the secrets Quincie mentioned, and I'm the one she chose to trust with it.

As the girls cover Quincie's body, I set the sword on the roof of the car. I draw and, unleashing the safety, give my tranq gun to Kayla and my Taser gun to Jess. "Whoever the retrieval teams can spare should be on their way. Jess, can you—?"

"I'll wait here for them." Jess pulls out her phone. "In the meantime, this is still my daddy's jurisdiction. I've got to let him know what's happening . . . before he misses the car."

Kayla and I take off running, across the manicured grass around the hotel, past swaths of wildflowers, to the amphitheater. She pulls ahead at the horse and donkey corral.

Her speed—it's breathtaking. She reaches the amphitheater before I do.

KAYLA

DUCKING BEHIND a heavy canvas arch, I can't see past the frenzied mid-shift crowd.

I leap for the nearest metal rafter, scanning for Clyde. There, center stage! He's cut up badly. His face is a bloody mess. He's staring at his hands as if he doesn't know what they are.

Is that woman sprawled next to him the governor? Is she *dead*? I aim the tranquilizer gun.

Aimee is close enough to a mic for it to pick up her voice. "It's too risky to wait any longer. You're all off camera. Leave now and there'll be no proof you were ever here."

I fire. The dart strikes Clyde's hip. Arching his back, he growls in surprise.

Seth's head rises, and he meets my eyes. "Guards!"

Before the yetis can get me in their sights, I drop into a crouch, vault down the center aisle. I'm a blur against the noisy crowd. "Clyde!" I shout. "Clyde, stop!"

"It's all about to come crashing down." Aimee's voice again. "Daemon Island all over again. Let Seth take the blame."

As I pass, the female yeti — Crystal — draws a revolver from her baby's sling and points it at the male who's running the tech. "Move away from the controls!" Then she waves away the henchman holding Aimee at gunpoint. "Retreat to the helipad. Guards, retreat!"

"Clyde!" I yell, approaching. He doesn't seem to recognize his name. "What're you —?"

His first blow knocks the tranq gun out of my hands. Then his Lion claws tear the bottom of my shirt, raking across my stomach. I gasp. I'm cut, bleeding, springing back on reflex to avoid being hurt worse. Oh, boy . . . I don't think Clyde's in there anymore.

"Give that gun to me!" the male yeti shouts. "You're hysterical. Your hormones —"

"So help me, Boreal, if you explain my hormones to me one more time, I will shoot you!"

Seth whips his head in her direction. "You are nothing,

YOSHI

I LAND PAST Clyde and Kayla, on the far opposite side of the stage from Seth.

I'm sore, frustrated, seeing spots. Fighting the urge to go full Cat, I push to my feet. A werehyena makes a grab for my throat, and I smack him aside. A werebuffalo thunders over the Hyena, crashing against me. God, he's heavy!

The stampede turns into a tangled pileup. I glimpse Kayla, ducking under the blue curtain. My nose identifies one of the Bears as Tanya. Where's the sword?

In their scramble to rip us "asunder" (seriously, who talks like that?), the chipped shifters are wrestling each another in competition to be the one who gets to do the ripping. In the confusion, I manage to squeeze free between

Crystal. *Nothing.* You're only here because your thick-headed mate —" She fires, shearing off one of the demon's horns.

The lights on the cameras are still shining. They're still broadcasting.

Not good. To the millions watching, the demon is projecting a megalomaniacal, mentally unhinged weresnake, and the homicidal Lion king is threatening a teenage girl. Not just any girl, but me, the alleged Cat girl of Pine Ridge.

The yetis are still bickering, but I'm too busy trying to stay alive to pay close attention. I don't know how much of the tranquilizer got into Clyde's system, but he apparently had enough presence of mind to pull out the dart. Backing away, I trip over Lawson and my torn stomach muscles spasm. It would make all the difference if I showed my fur, if I showed myself — an *Acinonyx jubatus sapiens* — battling the Lion who murdered the governor.

Humanity would see that we shifters aren't united against them.

Clyde circles the body, stalking me. He staggers and shakes his head. I scramble farther away, between two of the columns and, flailing, into the blue backdrop.

If I shift, that will confirm the park video. This isn't some small-town skirmish, captured in low light, framed in conflicting stories. I'll be publicly verified as a werecat.

On the other hand, if I can stay alive in human form, people will assume I'm a regular girl. The way Clyde's bearing down, anybody with teeth and claws of her own would use them.

It takes all the willpower I possess to stop my inner Cat from defending herself. My hand connects with something solid behind the shiny material. I reach under it to pull out a bright orange juggling pin. I heave it in Clyde's direction, narrowly missing his head.

I'm not ashamed of what I am. I just never wanted to pay the price of other people's ignorance. But then, how can they be expected to appreciate the full truth of Kayla, if it's always hidden? When we whispered our final good-byes, Ben's ghost said he wanted to celebrate me.

Everybody should feel the same. I thought I'd come to terms with that, but the past week tested my resolve. It was one thing to own my species before I became a celebrity, before the threat of war, before guns and demons and living in fear. The answer is what it always is: faith.

I miss my moment. Above, Yoshi leaps from one rafter to the next, cheating with a . . . it's a trapeze. He releases his black fur, raising Quincie's sword high above his head.

Careening downward, he swings the blade, slicing off one of Seth's fangs. It crashes onto the stage, leaving a strange, smoky trail in its wake. The bellowing demon's tail swats Yoshi's torso, sending him flying back at the rafters. Yoshi's shoulder hits metal. The weapon falls from his hands. The amphitheater is bursting with discord. Does the demon care how he achieves his goal, or is this what he wanted all along?

Seth booms, "Werebeasts, rip them asunder!"

a mountain weregoat wrestling with a pygmy weremammoth and a weredolphin who can't be happy this far from the ocean.

At the same moment, Clyde somehow escapes, only to knock me down again. He's ragged from the whip, and we're both riddled with oozing claw marks.

Oh, God. Oh, boy, I remember what it's like, when the animal form takes over and you're tempted to eat your big sister's fancy chickens. I saw it in Teghan's wild eyes on Daemon Island. Letting her weredevil run free helped her to survive.

I sense the inner war, man versus Lion, inside Clyde.

He's pinned me down, and having a Lion's bulk gives him the advantage.

"Sorry, man!" I gasp. "You're a handsome guy, but my heart belongs to Kayla." His salivating jaws open, and I add, "Come on, you're *not* going to kill me." Then again, he did kill the governor only moments ago. "Clyde, you can fight this. I know you can." I play to his Lion's heartstrings. "You're one of my best friends."

I close my eyes against the pain to come . . . and it doesn't. I risk a peek.

The golden mane shakes, and Clyde squints at me. His face morphs to mid-shift Possum and back to mid-shift Lion again. "I am? *I'm* one of your best friends? That's sad, Yoshi. It really is. I don't even like you."

"Don't be ridiculous. *Everybody* likes me." For worse

and better, he's Clyde again. I shove him off. "Your breath smells awful."

Shrugging off a werelemur, he gives me a hand up. "It's the weirdest thing. Lawson tasted like charcoaled crap." He sounds more confused than grief-stricken. It hasn't sunk in yet that he took the governor's life or what that will mean for all of us.

I, for one, have no desire to go to war against the human race.

I punch an Armadillo. We're in defense mode, battling back-to-back. Between the full-bodied Elk, Bear, and Buffalo, I can't see Seth, Aimee, or Kayla.

Breathing hard, Clyde asks, "Where's Quincie?"

I hate having to tell him. "I'm sorry, man. She didn't make it."

"What?" Clyde asks, shoving aside a weresloth. "She . . . how? Fire? Beheading?"

I deliver a roundhouse kick to a Wolf. "Her head — it's still on, but she hit the back of it on a rock. Hard." My own shoulder is still throbbing. It must be shock. We're talking about the death of one of Clyde's closest friends, and he seems to be taking it in stride. "Do you get what I'm saying? She had no pulse. Quincie's —"

"Oh!" the Wild Card exclaims. "Right, that's too bad. I . . . I have sadness over my dead friend. I'm, uh, grieving and sorrowful. Um, did you happen to notice a sword?"

AIMEE

"CRYSTAL!" I shove myself between her and Boreal, past caring about the revolver. Baby Drifa is wailing at the top of her lungs. "Call off the mob! I'm begging you. Please!"

Ignoring me, Boreal says, "We can salvage this. All the home audience will see is shifters as savages." The baby hiccups as he adds, "They'll be lining up to order from MCC Enterprises."

Thank you for that sound bite! Crystal realizes it before he does. Her fist pounds the button controlling the mic on the media console. "To the helipad — now."

That's it for Boreal. He retreats through the manic midshift crowd. "Your status falls with mine!" he calls after her. "You'll be barred for life from the Assembly of Matrons."

Crystal puts the, I assume, loaded gun back in the sling with her baby. I swear, she's as bad of a parent as my dad.

"Boreal speaks true," she informs me, stroking Drifa's furry white forehead. "She and I both will suffer disgrace. Unless . . ." Her voice grows more urgent. "You must tell me, pet. Where is Junior? We can still —"

"You can't have Junior," I say. "You can't kill or contain him, and you can't kill or contain everyone who's met him . . . or one of your species. Every shifter here —"

"Those beasts . . ." She gestures to the stage, where the mob is attacking my friends. "At least those who'll survive, they have been programmed to forget having ever seen a *Homo deific.*"

How convenient. "But the centuries-old organization that's protecting Junior right now, that's a different story. Believe me, there's no way my friends would've come here tonight without serious backup." Please, God, let that be true for a change. "Tell me how to call off the mob, and I'll argue to the interfaith coalition that it's wrong to out *Homo deific* to the world."

It's not much, the promise of an argument from a teenage human girl, but it's the best offer she's going to get. I add, "Or you could stick around and see if you end up on a dissection table or caged in a zoo." We can hear the helicopter start up outside, waiting.

"Well played, pet," Crystal replies, lumbering off with

her newborn. Over her shoulder, she yells, "The control word is *werebeasts!*"

Finally! "Werebeasts!" That didn't do anything. I punch the mic button on the console and try again. "Werebeasts, forget about the Cats and the Lion. I mean, Lossum. I mean, Clyde!"

The mob pauses, disengaging from the fray. "Sorry, I would never say 'werebeasts' normally. I had no choice!" Gah! They could care less right now. Think, Aimee. What do I want them to do? "Uh, move out, exit through the back of the amphitheater. Keep your horns, hooves, and claws to yourselves. Avoid the evil giant demon snake — watch out for his fangs, fang. Pay no attention to the snowpeople fleeing by helicopter. Thank you for your cooperation. Have a nice night."

KAYLA

THE LAST YETI is out of here, and Seth slinks behind the blue backdrop, exiting too. Now that the shifter crowd has thinned, I'm able to spot where Yoshi dropped the sword. I leap from a rafter to catch the nearest trapeze and swing, letting go to retrieve the sword and run after the demon.

Against my palm, the weapon feels reassuring. All that time my minister was droning on about the horrors of werepeople, he could've been giving his congregation useful demon-slaying tips. Just saying. I guess I'll have to wing it.

I pour on the speed and, using both hands, sink the blade deep into Seth's thick tail. His triangular head nudges into view through the material. "You, again!" Seth snaps at my arms, and I let go. Suddenly, the sword is on fire. *Why* is it on fire? *How* is it on fire?

Bonus, the demon is on fire, too. He's thrashing, trying to free himself. His jaws make a pass at the hilt, and he recoils. "Help me!" he calls, panicked. "Holy fire!" His voice has lost its haughtiness. He sounds plaintive, vulnerable. That was easier than I expected. He screams it again, more desperate. "Holy fire!"

At first, I thought it was an exclamation. Like "Holy fire, Batman!" But no, he means the fire is holy, as in blessed, divine. That's why the sliced-off fang began smoking, smoldering, too. Only . . . who does Seth think he's talking to?

I can hear the helicopter taking off. His allies are out of here.

"Kayla!" Yoshi grabs my hand. "Your wound, shift it out."

Oh. I almost forgot. Adrenaline, I guess. Usually, shifts take their own course. I struggle to concentrate on that one area.

Seth writhes, spewing black-and-blue smoke. Again he bellows, "Holy fire!"

Clyde pulls us both out of the way. "Give the monster room to burn."

I've partly knitted my skin, but it's tough going. I'm light-headed from the effort and blood loss. The amphitheater has cleared out. It's all but over.

257

"The governor!" Aimee shouts, joining us onstage. "She's —"

"Nothing can help her now." I notice the mic hanging from a rafter above and realize I probably shouldn't have said that. Are the cameras still broadcasting? This is Texas. Clyde killed the governor on live TV. He'll definitely get the death penalty.

"No!" Aimee shouts, pointing over her boyfriend's shoulder. "Behind you!"

Oh, sweet baby Jesus. It's Governor "Laughin' Linnie" Lawson. Her throat and face are a mess of meat. She's lurching in our direction.

"Zombie?" Clyde reaches into the pocket of his harem pants and hits a key on his phone. "Uh, what do we know about zombies?"

AIMEE

"NO WORRIES," Clyde says, pocketing his phone again. "Kieren says zombies just shuffle around and moan. We can forget . . . uh-oh."

Triangle patterns appear around the governor's eyes; her ears extend into horns. Her head flattens and widens, causing her tall light-brown wig to topple. Her red suit splits at the seams, and her taupe pumps fall away as she transforms from woman to snake. Another shape-changer, another demon like Seth. They look exactly alike, except her eyes are a milky yellow, not orange. She exclaims, "What have you done to Daddy?"

"Not a zombie," Clyde concludes.

Yoshi lunges for the sword and dislodges it from Seth's tail, severing the flaming part from the rest of him. What remains is scorched but no longer on fire.

Yoshi glances at the now-glowing weapon in his hand like he's not sure he made the right call. Two demons, one holy sword. He swings wide at Lawson's gyrating torso, mindful of her descending fangs. Meanwhile, Seth gives up pretending to be a weresnake, and before we know it, both demons are two, no, three times their initial size, nearly thirty feet tall. Seth's headset mic has snapped in half and come tumbling off. He's still lightning fast, but still down to one fang, one horn. He looks lopsided, and he's off-balance on his tail stub.

"Why didn't you help me?" Seth exclaims, dancing to avoid Yoshi's blade. "I could've been destroyed by holy flame!" The demons slither around us. "I'll be the punch line at every comedy club in Lucifer's capital city!"

"I was busy." Lawson captures me in her tail. "I was pretending to be dead!"

I'm lifted off my feet as Seth informs his spawn, "I was screaming 'holy fire'! You have to learn to pay attention. We don't excuse ADD in hell!"

I can hear my friends yelling my name, cursing the demons.

"But I was doing such a good job." Lawson swings her head so we're nose to nose. Her breath is rank. Her eyes are gleaming. I could reach out and caress her horns. She adds, "I fooled all of them. I could've been president of the United States someday!" Then, noticing the crosses tattooed around my neck, she jerks back. Her grip tightens, squeezing air from my lungs.

"A demon world leader?" Seth mocks. "How unoriginal! Have you never heard of Ivan the Terrible, Idi Amin, Andrew Jackson? It's like your banal circus concept all over again."

Lawson tries to defend herself. "Boreal liked —"

"Boreal doesn't matter," Seth rants on. "The aborted police sweeps, the FHPU, it's been one mess after another with you."

Trying to save me, Clyde leaps to rake his claws down Lawson's scaly belly. "Retract your fur!" I choke out. "Show your crosses! Show —"

Seth pierces Clyde's shoulder with his poisonous fang.

261

KAYLA

YOSHI NICKS LAWSON with the sword. The demon wails. Flames *whoosh* up. "Aimee!"

Yoshi's knees buckle. He'd been trying to save her. Instead, she's lost to the blaze.

Clyde's been impaled, poisoned. The demons give us no chance to grieve. Yoshi struggles to hold them both at bay while covering me. He slices Lawson's torso, separating Aimee in hopes the flames will dissipate. They do, but too late.

We've got to end this now. "Yoshi, give me a boost!"

He holds out his free hand. I step up and, with his added muscle, leap again to an overhead trapeze. Only this time I'm on camera. It's a showy move.

Tonight we're heaven's foot soldiers, battling hell spawn with holy fire. "Hey, Seth!" I shout, swinging back and forth. "Seth, I'll make you a deal."

Yoshi pivots with the sword to block Lawson's fangs, and I drop onto her back, where her head narrows to tail. As she bucks, I sink in my left claws to hang on. "Yoshi, the sword!"

He tosses the weapon, hilt first, to me, and I stretch to make the catch, right-handed.

Yoshi's defenseless now. I've got to make this work.

I rest the edge of the blade against Lawson's blotchy scales. They smolder. "What are you doing?" she exclaims. "What have you done to my alluring tail?"

Snake demons trade in children? Time to talk to Seth about his. "Seth," I begin again. "If you never again target, torment, or even annoy shifters, *Homo sapiens*, or . . ." Why not? "Any closely related species, then I won't behead Lawson."

"That's *not* my name," she pipes up like it's important at the moment. "Let history show I am Til'tehxya, Intern of Discord. Disguised as Lawson, I have endured nagging media and blah chicken dinners, and no matter what incantation I try, I always get a run in my panty hose."

"Go ahead," Seth says. "Behead her." Beneath my thighs, I feel Til's scales adjust in response. He adds, "She's whiny, always making excuses, and I have fifty thousand more spawn roaming Lucifer's capital, including a favored eighteen who've been admitted to university." He sounds sincerely proud of that, like it's on the bumper sticker of his hell mobile. "Two Chaos majors, three in Bigotry, one in Culinary Arts, and a dozen in Negative Self-Esteem."

"Culinary Arts?" Yoshi echoes. He's kneeling by Clyde, who's reaching toward the smoky fire that's consumed Aimee.

"Everybody's got to eat," Seth quips. "Counteroffer: Let me go. Call off your second front outside the amphitheater, and I'll leave *Homo sapiens, Homo shifters,* and *Homo deific* to create discord wholly of their own making. You hardly need my help anyway."

We've already lost Aimee and Quincie, too. We have to get Clyde to a healer. My stomach clenches, and the skin breaks again. "It's a deal," I announce. "You can go."

As Seth shoots out of the amphitheater, Til tries once more to buck me off. "We can talk about this," she pleads. "We can make a deal. Do you have a pet? A kitten or puppy? I'd be happy to talk about —"

Puppy? The blade bursts into flames as I shove it through her reptilian neck. No way is that satanic freak going anywhere near Peso.

YOSHI

LAWSON'S SEVERED HEAD smacks the ground, and Kayla leaps, graceful, to my side. She uses the flaming sword to split Lawson's pale belly from the base to the charred tip of her tail. Then Kayla rushes to what remains of Seth's flesh around Aimee's body.

"Aimee," Clyde gasps. "Get her away from that thing."

His Lion-form face dissolves to human, his expression contorted in pain. I snatch a scrap of fallen red linen that used to be the governor's lapel. "All clear," I say into the mic. "Forget the fleeing monster. We need a healer — now!" We need more than that — an incantation, a full-blown spell.

Whatever works, or we're going to lose Clyde, too.

Kayla returns the sword to me and uses her bare hands to tear ashy demon meat from Aimee's face. "It's not hot. She's not burned." The Cat girl sounds mystified. "She's alive!"

"Tell Aimee . . ." Clyde's eyelids flutter shut. "Tell her . . ."

His blood has bloomed to cover his heart.

"Tell her *what*?" I ask, grasping his hand. "Come on, man. Stay with me."

The medical team swarms in, their identities protected by masks, and we're pushed out of the way. Mrs. Morales mutters, "We've got no antivenom for that thing." She kneels. *"Clyde!"*

"What?" Aimee's voice sounds soft and small. Kayla helps her to her feet.

Holding each other, we watch and wait, helpless.

"She saved him last time," Aimee whispers. "Miz Morales brought him out of the coma." In the months since, Clyde has lived a lifetime. He found passion in Noelle, love in Aimee, and not only the Lion but the man within. On the biggest, best adventures of my life, Clyde was the guy by my side.

Mrs. Morales looks up at us through tears and shakes her head. Aimee collapses against me. I hate that the world's watching. I call, "Cut the transmission."

"No," Kayla says. "Don't. Clyde died *pretending* to be somebody else, and the demons used it against him. Don't you see? The problem isn't who and what we are. It's the lies, the apologies, the pretenses . . . No matter the consequences, God made us this way. We're glorious."

Before I can stop her, the Cat girl steps up to address the cameras. "Hello, world. My name is Kayla Morgan. I'm from Pine Ridge, Texas, and I'm a werecat. An *Acinonyx jubatus sapiens*. You've seen me before on TV or on the Internet.

"I'm sure you're confused, possibly even frightened. That's because you don't understand. Listen to me. I'm going to explain what just happened. I'm going to explain the difference between a horror and a hero."

GOD ALMIGHTY
The Sword of Swords
The Big Boss

To: Zachary
cc: Michael
From: God
Date: Monday, April 28

The necessity of secrecy on the part of angelic forces in affecting events on the mortal plane has been emphasized to you since the dawn of your existence.

Nevertheless, you relinquished your sword to your former assignment, the vampire Quincie P. Morris, to surreptitiously execute a hell-spawn demon in Bastrop County, Texas.

She failed to do so. Instead, in an entirely foreseeable chain of events, five hundred million living souls (and counting) have witnessed werecats Kayla Morgan and Yoshi Kitahara sequentially wielding said weapon to destroy one hell spawn and to battle another to a draw.

Consequently, on every continent of earth, the status of werepeople as my blessed children, the holy nature of your sword, the role of faith, and the ongoing threat posed by the demonic are competing for most prevalent topic of mortal thought and conversation.

Thank you for making my job more interesting.

Well done.

CLYDE

I DIED. It sucks. I never had the chance to put together a bucket list, let alone check stuff off of it. But because I've got unfinished business, I've decided to stick around.

They're haunted people — Yoshi, Kayla, and especially Aimee — haunted by me.

Dr. Morales figured out how to use the tracking function of the brain chips to pick up the remaining shifters in the woods. Now they're all at the makeshift medical bay at the B&B in Pine Ridge. After healing up from the extractions, they'll be sent home or someplace safer.

After a quick debate, the grown-ups took a sample of Seth's charred remains for study. They left the rest for humanity to figure out (or not) for itself.

Jess's dad, Sheriff Bigheart, was the first non-coalition cop on the scene. Arriving in his wife's hot-pink VW Beetle, he beat the SWAT team by three minutes.

Kayla insisted on staying, after the coalition pulled out, to answer media questions. Yoshi stood by her. When Mayor and Mrs. Morgan arrived twenty minutes later, they did, too.

Detectives Zaleski and Wertheimer spoke on behalf of the kidnapped shifters.

Father Ramos explained the demons and calmed public hysteria, but only after calming down himself when Kayla and Yoshi presented him with Zachary's holy sword for safekeeping. That took a few minutes of deep breathing and a shot of Freddy's 192-proof Polish vodka.

Meanwhile, Freddy started publicly releasing some of Graham Barnard's computer files. They verified MCC Enterprises' involvement ("at the highest levels") in "the incident" and set off an international debate on legal protections for werepeople.

Nobody mentioned the *Homo deific* to any of the outside cops or the press.

CLYDE

AT THE B&B, the medics scrubbed the blood off my body. They changed me back into my blue jeans and Sanguini's logo T-shirt. They returned Leander's watch to Noelle.

My body was laid out in the living room of the main house. It was surrounded by blue glass vases filled with fresh-picked wildflowers.

I locate Aimee resting alone in a small log cabin on the property. She's propped on lacy pillows. She's staring off into space on a twin-size brass bed. Her wrist is bandaged. She's ignoring the cup of tea on the nightstand.

I'm debating whether to materialize when someone knocks.

"Aimee?" It's Junior. He opens the front door a crack.

No response.

Junior tilts his huge furry head. He shuffles in carrying his enormous white cat, Blizzard. "Your dad is asking if you'll see him." He sets the cat on the bed. After kneading the quilt, it stretches — theatrically — over Aimee's lap and purrs. Her fingers curl into the white fur.

"Freddy called your mom," Junior adds. "She's on her way." He takes the rustic rocking chair beside the end table. "I like it here," he says. "Reminds me of Granny Z's cabin."

No response. I have to give Junior credit. He keeps trying. "I'm sorry about Clyde. Your dad is outside. He wants to know if he can come in."

Aimee yanks off her sweet-sixteen ring. She tosses it out an open window.

I guess that answers that. Scratching Blizzard's chin, she says, "The way I see it, once somebody offers their kid as collateral in a bargain with scaly horned hell spawn who kills her beloved Lossom, then adios to bedside chats." Moments later, she reaches for Junior's hand. "If you want, you can live in the hideout house, hang out with my friends, and wash dishes at Sanguini's with me."

"Like a normal person?" he asks. "With a normal job? How is that possible?"

"All I have to do is ask. Nobody's going to say no to me today." It's only a wisp of a smile, but it's there. "The neighbors will get used to you, and everyone at the restaurant will think you're a cosplay genius. Trust me, Austin loves the weird."

272

CLYDE

NEARLY TWO WEEKS LATER, Yoshi secures the newly replaced lock on the front door of Austin Antiques. He's decked out in a black tux with a white bow tie and vest. He looks like a Eurasian James Bond. Still pissed that his grandmother made him work today, he messages Kayla to say he's on his way to Pine Ridge.

He's Mr. Relationship. I haven't caught him scoping out another girl. Not even when bombshell Quandra Perez strolled into the antiques mall with her mother.

He's doubled down at school. He joined Aimee's tae kwon do class. He's lifting weights at five every morning with his sister.

"My, don't you look dashing!" Chef Nora surprises Yoshi in front of the Bone Chiller, the SUV that used to be mine. The car is covered in dominoes made from the bones of shape-shifters (an eBay purchase). I donated it months ago to the interfaith coalition.

It's a huge deal for Nora to abandon Sanguini's kitchen this close to sundown on a Saturday. She's still wearing her uniform, complete with kitchen clogs.

"Nora!" Yoshi gives her a hug. "Uh, what're you doing here?" He runs his palm across the hood. "This is . . . was Clyde's car." He's on the verge of getting choked up again. He was a mess at my funeral. Cried baby-man tears. It was awesome.

Nora presses forward. "Those of us at the coalition thought you might need it for tonight's mission." It's the first time I've heard her admit she's more than "in touch" with the organization. She's part of it.

Yoshi opens his mouth and closes it again. "Tonight?"

Obviously, the guy's got plans.

Nora chuckles. "We're offering you an official field position, hon. You're going to graduate from high school in a couple of weeks. You've proven yourself a cool Cat under pressure, and you come highly recommended by an emeritus operative."

The chef slips the SUV keys into his palm. His gaze falls on the manila-colored brick antiques mall that used to be his only future. "Me?"

"I'll take that as a yes," Nora says. "It won't be easy. You'll be trained in disguise, languages, combat, weapons, diplomacy . . . And right now this vehicle's too flashy, but that's nothing some paint can't fix." Flashy, my bald Possum tail.

"Speaking for myself, I think you've got a bright future in enchanted antiquities," Nora adds. "But that's not tonight's mission."

Nora is southern reasonableness personified. She's old enough that arguing with her seems disrespectful. But Yoshi's got a girlfriend to answer to. "What *is* tonight's mission?"

Nora opens the driver's door for him. "Pine Ridge prom."

CLYDE

THE VETERAN'S CENTER in Pine Ridge has morphed into Morgan campaign headquarters. Kayla's dad is running for governor.

Last Thursday the body of the *real* Linnie Lawson was discovered. It was found by a construction company in the process of rehabbing a ratty-looking strip mall. She'd been folded into a freezer found in the back of a mom-and-pop pharmacy. The place had been stocked with MCC Injections' shift-suppressing vaccine and patches.

According to the autopsy, the governor died in early February. She was poisoned with venom that couldn't be matched to any known animal species. Sound familiar?

At Morgan campaign central, I spot a few familiar faces. They're seated at long foldout tables. They're stuffing envelopes and drinking coffee. The werewolf newlyweds from Daemon Island are wearing Thing One and Thing Two T-shirts from their honeymoon in Orlando. Closest to the stage, Mei is talking to Mrs. Morales about apprenticing as a healer. Her husband, James, is chatting up Dr. Morales about becoming an engineering graduate assistant.

At the next table, Sheriff Bigheart is comparing notes with Detective Zaleski on the "snake of unusual size" spotted yesterday in Lady Bird Lake.

Yoshi's grandmother is bitching to Eleanora Stubblefield about the deviled eggs served after her twin sister Lula's funeral. It was last weekend, the day before mine. At my funeral, Ms. Kitahara bitched to my parents about the music, performed live by the Brazos Boys.

After I found out I was, as Aimee says, a Lossum, I wondered if I was a reminder to my parents of their rocky times. I was an idiot. They're still tearing up at how Pop-Pop Richards insisted on paying for my send-off. He had me buried in the Armadillo royal family plot next to Travis at Magnolia Shade Cemetery. Leander didn't show up at all, but my name was inscribed in *The Book of Lions* as a prince of the Pride.

It's not easy, growing up Possum. I'm no angel, but I'll watch over Clara, Claudette, Cleatus, and Clint every day for the rest of their lives.

Onstage in Pine Ridge, the mayor/gubernatorial candidate is leaning forward in a brown-and-white cowhide chair. It's on loan from Stubblefield's Secrets on Main.

A *Capital City News* reporter is poised in a matching chair across from him. She double-checks her voice recorder. "In light of her heroism during the Whispering Pines calamity, your adopted daughter has become a household name."

That's what the media is calling it, "a calamity." They're trying to sound southwest-y.

She goes on, "But do you think Texans are ready to elect a werecat's parent, even if he's human, to the state's highest office?"

"First off, Kayla is my daughter — period. No qualifications." Mayor Morgan stands and buttons his jacket as Kayla and Yoshi make their entrance. "Second, that's a conversation with the people of Texas that I'm looking forward to. If you'll excuse me for a moment . . ."

Kayla dyed her hair dark again. She's rocking a strapless, backless sequined gown — it's royal blue with a rhinestone belt. She's wearing a cat's-eye gemstone necklace. It's the one she gave to Ben on Valentine's Day. It was retrieved from the carousel by Sheriff Bigheart.

Kayla and Yoshi are meeting Jess and Brenek (it's a setup) at Lurie's Steakhouse. They'll continue to Pine Ridge prom at the opera house. Then they'll cruise to Austin to party on at Sanguini's. It's Waterloo High prom night, too.

Kayla's had an intense couple of weeks. She's the cover girl on the inaugural issue of *Shifter Scene* magazine. Cal Tech took out a full-page ad in support of her in the *New York Times*. But her family had to change churches. There's talk of stripping her state championships in track and cross-country. The National Council for Preserving Humanity staged a protest during Lula's burial (they were drowned out by the PRHS marching band).

Coffee in hand, Ms. Kitahara moseys across the room. "I hear you've got a solid lead on that blasted shifter-human trafficking ring."

Freddy is marking counties with color-coded pushpins on a mounted map of Texas. "And I hear you wrote the most glowing recommendation in the history of the interfaith coalition for your grandson."

She uses a purple pushpin to mark Austin Antiques. "Yoshi doesn't much care for me. Ruby says if I don't make it better, I'll lose them both."

Good for Ruby. Kayla went to Freddy and Nora about Ms. Kitahara's gun-happy temper. They suggested Yoshi move in to the hideout house with Junior and his cat. You know, to watch over the arctic ass — I mean, to keep the kid company.

Across the hall, campaign volunteers *ooh* and *ahh* at the young Cats in formal attire. This a staged photo op.

The *Capital City News* videographer scrambles to take full advantage. Most of the room draws out their handhelds, which flash as they take pics of their own.

Mayor Morgan makes a show of shaking Yoshi's hand. He leans in to kiss Kayla on the cheek. "You sure about all this, pumpkin?"

Her smile is spectacular. "Bring it."

~ᴇ Sanguini's ᴇ~

A VERY RARE RESTAURANT

PROM AFTER-PARTY MENU

prey antipasto

green, black, and kalamata olives roasted in olive oil
with garlic, herbs, and Italian bread

goat cheese and avocado–stuffed Roma tomatoes

prey dolce

zeppole with vanilla ice cream

predator antipasto

shrimp and catfish quenelles with white wine sauce

chicken-fried rabbit's foot and
miniature blood waffles with lingonberry syrup

predator dolce

candied bacon and lobster ice cream

CLYDE

HOURS LATER Yoshi picks up Kieren at the Morales McMansion for the after-party at Sanguini's. The Wolf has recovered enough to shift out most of his injuries. He's still sore and moving slowly.

He and Quincie skipped the big dance. They're not really the prom types. Neither is Yoshi, but Kayla was born for that sort of thing. Where she goes, he follows.

At Sanguini's the teenage crowd looks grown-up. They're swaying to a three-piece string band. Noelle is stylin' in a slinky, low-cut black dress. She's singing "Strangers in the Night."

Yani, the hostess, leads my friends across the dark blue carpeting to their table.

The expediter Jamal announces that Quincie will join them in a moment. Without bothering to ask, he drops off two orders of each of the predator appetizers. "Compliments of Chef Nora."

The official story is that Quincie was knocked unconscious when she fell and hit her head (that's true). The tranquilizer — at shifter dosage — slowed down her metabolism to the point that Yoshi couldn't detect a pulse (that's not).

Jess is a first-timer at the restaurant. She spears a chicken-fried rabbit's foot and pops it into her mouth. Her eyes widen. She covers her lips. "We'll need another order of this."

"You're already hungry again?" Brenek cracks his knuckles. As a werebear, he's charmed by the idea of a human girl with a healthy appetite.

"I like that one of us is driving the Bone Chiller," Kieren says to Yoshi. "But don't you already have a car?"

One of us? With me and Travis out of the picture, the Wolf could use a guy friend. Speaking of Travis, the archangel Michael mentioned that he and Zachary would be leading my welcome party when I reach "the reunion desk of the Penultimate." I'm not sure what all that means. I'm almost ready to find out. Almost.

Another angel, the miraculously recovered guardian Joshua, salutes me from the service station. When this is over, he's on deck to comfort anyone who needs to talk.

Yoshi puts his arm around Kayla. "The Chiller is enormous, and I've got more people in my life now." The Cat says that like it's a revelation. After growing up on a Kansas farm with only his big sis for company, I guess it is.

He adds, "It's like how Wonder Woman can carry a passenger or two, but to transport half the Justice League, she needs her invisible plane."

"What did you say?" Aimee asks, coming up behind him with Quincie. She's adorably sweaty. Her turquoise-streaked blond curls are a mess. She's been washing dishes in the kitchen with Junior. "About Wonder Woman and the plane?"

The Cat blushes. He runs his hand over his face.

Kayla nudges him with her elbow. "Got you."

That's my cue. "I've obviously been a good influence on him." The light is low, flickering. I appear corporeal enough to anyone not looking too closely. I've chosen to show myself in an AWESOME POSSUM T-shirt and faded jeans, like I've been washing dishes, too.

At the mic, Noelle stumbles over the lyrics of "Fly Me to the Moon." Can the crowd see me? I don't think so. Other than my friends, no one reacts.

We're in the slipstream between earth and the celestial plane. I don't need my shifter instincts to read their feelings. It's in the way they hold themselves and one another. It's in every memory we've already made.

Aimee marches right up. "About the DCU animated series —"

"About the online RPGs," I reply, upping the ante. We never got around to discussing the superhero animated series. There was always too much to say about graphic novels and live-action films and TV. Skipping to online role-playing games, that's reckless. Crazy.

It's how we express our true feelings.

"RPGs, huh?" Aimee reaches for my hand, but her fingers slip through. She falters, tangled in grief. She lowers her head, nodding. "Okay, Lossum. Dazzle me."

"Look up," I whisper, shape-shifting one last time.

My mane unfurls in black-and-blue butterflies. It's a glimpse of heaven.

My tribute to our love and the heroes we've become.

Dazzling.

AUTHOR'S NOTE

Feral Pride is the roaring finale of a trilogy that includes *Feral Nights* and *Feral Curse*. The books are set in the same fantastical universe as my Tantalize series, which features Quincie, Kieren, Zachary, and Miranda as co-protagonists and is made up of *Tantalize, Eternal, Blessed,* and *Diabolical,* as well as two graphic novels, *Tantalize: Kieren's Story* and *Eternal: Zachary's Story,* both gorgeously illustrated by Ming Doyle. Several characters, settings, and mythologies overlap.

Together, the Feral and Tantalize series take place over the course of one fictional academic school year. In reality, from draft one of book one to the release of *Feral Pride,* the journey was fifteen years. If I could go back in time and tell my inner fifteen-year-old that someday she would grow up and get to do this as her job, she would've been spinning over the moon.

Much is owed to the readers whose questions about the early books inspired my writing the later ones. If you're new to the universe, all the novels can stand alone, although *Tantalize* and *Blessed* are best appreciated in concert and *Feral Pride* is clearly crafted as a finale.

The incident involving Zachary and the minor hell-spawn Duane in Austin's downtown Whole Foods parking lot is brought to life in my short story "Cupid's Beaux," which is centered on the guardian angel Joshua. Other short stories set in the universe include "Haunted Love" and "Cat Calls."

Returning to *Feral Pride*, the Bigheart name is Osage and used with permission of the real-life Bigheart family in Austin. However, none of the fantasy elements in either series are drawn from Native American belief systems or traditional stories.

I unabashedly admit taking some serious liberties with the Austin Police Department, the Bastrop County Sheriff's Office, the California Institute of Technology, and the Texas Department of Safety. Along those same lines, to my knowledge, the Austin Zoo & Animal Sanctuary is not staffed by werecoyotes.

More wholly fictional elements include make-believe businesses, locales, media outlets, and publications such as *The Archangels' Code of Conduct*, Austin Antiques, Austin News Channel, *Bastrop County Examiner*, Bikes & Babes, *The Blood Drinker's Guide*, *The Book of Lions*, the Brazos Boys, *Capital City News*, Catchup, Daemon Island, Donna's Diner, Fayard & the French Horns, the International News Network, MCC Enterprises (and its subsidiaries), the city of Pine Ridge, the Screaming Head Colds, *Shifter Scene, Southwestern Cuisine*, the *Texas Talker*, Tia Leticia's Salsa Bar, and Whispering Pines Resort.

This is the point in these notes where I usually admit, with some regret, that Sanguini's: A Very Rare Restaurant is fictional, too. But this time I'll say this instead: If you're an investor and want to make Sanguini's a reality, have your people call my people. We'll see.

Finally, I do my best to track my literary, cinematic, pop cultural, historical, and other influences as I write. It's partly to pay tribute, partly to give credit, and perhaps most of all to remind myself that Story is all about connections and conversations that include me and each of you.

With that in mind, I respectfully nod to Neal Adams, Robert Angel, Kathi Appelt, K. A. Applegate, the Austin Independent Business Alliance, Dan Aykroyd, Francis Bacon, Donald P. Bellisario, E. Nelson Birdwell, Len Blum, Tim Burton, Robert Butler, Martin Caiden, Lorne Cameron, Stephen Carpenter, Cesar Chavez, Chris Chibnall, Ron Clements, Christina Crawford, Roald Dahl, Frank Darabont, Princess Diana of Wales, Paul Dini, Sir Arthur Conan Doyle, William Dozier, Ted Elliott, Tina Fey, Archduke Franz Ferdinand, Bill Finger, Ian Fleming, Gardner Fox, Mahatma Gandhi, Mark Gatiss, Michael Gleason, William Goldman, David Greenwalt, Monty Hall, Laurel K. Hamilton, Stefan Hatos, Don Heck, Michael Hirst, David Hoselton, John Hughes, Carmine Infantino, Joan of Arc, Kenneth Johnson, Bob Kane, Kellogg Company, Simon Kinberg, Rudyard Kipling, Jack Kirby, Karey Kirkpatrick, Eugene Kolkey, Jim Kouf, Eric Kripke, Guy Laliberté, Glen A. Larson, Stan Lee, Deborah Joy LeVine, C. S. Lewis, Larry Lieber, George Lucas, Niccolò Machiavelli, Elliot S. Maggin, Christopher Markus, William Moulton Marston, Stephen McFeely, Robert McKimson, Irene Mecchi, Steven Moffat, John Musker, George Orwell, Outhouse Designs,

George Papp, Zak Penn, Martin Provensen, Harold Ramis, Frank Robbins, Jonathan Roberts, Gene Roddenberry, Terry Rossio, Ernő Rubik, Haim Saban, Julius Schwartz, Jeffrey Scott, Dr. Seuss, William Shakespeare, Mary Shelley, Yuko Shimizu, Charles M. Shulz, Joe Shuster, Jerry Siegel, Joe Simon, Frank Sinatra, Gilles Ste-Croix, Abraham Stoker (the old master), Stephen Thompson, Bruce Timm, Toei Company, J. R. R. Tolkien, the Tudors, Gy Waldron, Red Wassenich, Morton Weisinger, David N. Weiss, Joss Whedon (the new master), Lee Ann Womack, Linda Woolverton, Cecily von Ziegesar, and Brian Yansky.

ACKNOWLEDGMENTS

Thanks to my editor, Deb, for keeping me on track on a thrilling ride that lasted longer than either of us expected. Thanks to my agent, Ginger, for securing my ticket to adventure. I likewise appreciate the efforts of all the fantastic — and perhaps fantastical — heroes at Candlewick Press, Walker Books, and Curtis Brown Ltd., especially Carter, Mina, Hilary, Andrea, Liz, Sharon, Erika, and Andie. Thanks to Greg Leitich Smith, who read every manuscript in the Tantalize and Feral series out loud, pen in hand, in our 1920s hideout house. At least twice.

My friends Donna Bowman Bratton, Carmen Oliver, Nancy Werlin, and Austin's awesome writing and illustration community (including expats and honorary members) assisted with research, helped brainstorm, and offered countless hugs and encouragement.

I also greatly appreciate the efforts and support of booksellers, teachers, librarians, bloggers, homeschoolers, and book-loving noisemakers (especially YAs) for making sure my novels found their readership.

All of you — or as we say in Texas, all y'all — are my heroes.